*A
Harlequin
Romance*

OTHER

Harlequin Romances

by MARGARET WAY

FLIGHT
INTO YESTERDAY

by

MARGARET WAY

Harlequin Books

TORONTO • LONDON • NEW YORK • AMSTERDAM • SYDNEY • WINNIPEG

Original hardcover edition published in 1976
by Mills & Boon Limited

ISBN 0-373-02016-3

Harlequin edition published October 1976

Printed in U.S.A.

CHAPTER ONE

He had come a long way to find this girl, and now that he had found her, he was angered by the force of his own reactions. She was lovely for one thing, dark-haired, smoky-eyed with a very white skin against the silky black mass of her hair. An ice-white camellia sprung vividly to life in front of him, yet he could only wait there silently condemning her.

They had never met, but he knew everything about her. His was no easy nor enviable position, cousin to Britt, Drew's friend and partner, and this girl had the distinction of taking up many long hours of his valuable time, doubly important for all of them with Drew in a wheelchair and so few commissions he could designate with any marked degree of confidence. Pressure lines formed themselves about his nose and his mouth and he found himself gripping the wheel just for something to catch hold of. This was the worst assignment in the world and one he had little taste for, but he had determined on it more than a month ago when Drew had his stroke. If this girl wouldn't come back with him of her own accord he would drag her off by force and violate all his own principles. He detested violence, yet the sight of her was arousing some pretty strong tensions. No one, especially a young girl, had the right to harbour such bitter enmity.

She was moving quickly towards him with a dancer's light, flowing motions, a kind of swaying from the narrow waist, the breeze sweeping her black hair around her face and whipping at the pleated print silk of her skirt. Her extreme slenderness and the faultless arrangement of her young limbs, her obvious delight in the tender magic of that spring afternoon created a picture of the most incredible innocence that he well knew was totally unreliable. At thirty-five the most singular thing he had learned about women was that their beauty was the greatest deception. Once he would have found it hard to credit that such bitterness and hostility could live in this patrician young creature, but he had lost all his most cherished illusions long ago. For all the perfection of her appearance, there was the far less alluring side of the coin. Britt's story was poignant enough without this new disaster of Drew's.

He was, he realised, quite taut with censure and he relaxed himself deliberately, lighting a cigarette and inhaling deeply, sending a jet of smoke through his nostrils. He was smoking too much lately. Overwork, too little sleep, anxiety over Drew, over the business, it all left its mark. Now this ... flower power. He knew it for what it was, and his handsome mouth hardened cynically. It was impossible to ignore her, but as an architect he supposed he could justify his own susceptibility to beauty. It had an hypnotic quality, then when he thought of the anguish Drew was enduring anger and antagonism hit him like a giant wave, mounting almost in rhythm with those carefree dancing movements until it seemed to be engulfing him. He swore gently and had himself under control in minutes. The one thing he had never been able to endure in a woman was vindictiveness, and this girl had the ugly trait in full measure. He might remember that when oddly, as now, the sight of her filled him with the greatest aesthetic pleasure.

She was blissfully unaware of him, her face lifted almost ecstatically to the blossoming bauhinias, delicate pink and white and cerise, starring both sides of the street and transforming it from something quite ordinary into a fairyland. On the surface, she couldn't have presented a more charming or innocent picture, but he wasn't deceived. He knew all her secrets, nevertheless it was difficult to reconcile the harsh facts with the youthful reality before him. The balance of credibility was overwhelmingly in her physical favour, yet Britt wouldn't lie and certainly not Drew, the girl's father. Nothing seemed to add up and he decided again, being a tenacious man, to find the key to her. Fastidious as well, it seemed almost an invasion of privacy for him to be so observing her at all without her knowledge and he swung out from behind the wheel of the car, slamming the door rather savagely and moving on to the grassy verge. Impatiently he willed her to catch sight of him. He loathed the whole thing, but it had to be got over. Drew was in pretty poor shape and this girl had to come up with the answers for whatever reason. If he couldn't appeal to some subterranean streak of compassion still left in her he was quite prepared to bribe her, and that in itself was making him over-react. He wondered what it would be like to strangle a woman with her own hair. Parked right outside her door as he was, he would have thought she would have taken note of it long before this. It didn't occur to him that she knew no one who could have aspired to his kind of car. All he could think of was that she was the best and the worst kind of woman. The type to linger in a man's memory so that it could become damned near impossible to exorcise the spell. This one had everything, except a heart. He considered himself lucky he had avoided marriage and saved himself one hell of a disappointment. Women! All they seemed to live for was revenge.

Natalie, abruptly, came out of her reverie as if she had stepped inside a magnetic field. A man was watching her and the whole world seemed changed, the radiance of the afternoon diminishing. Even at a distance she caught the steel in him, cut down by the clear contempt of his glance. His eyes were very blue and brilliant in a face of no compromise. Perfect sapphires, she thought ironically, and just as cold. Instinctively she came to a halt, her heart beating painfully, trying to mount some sort of defence for herself. Intuitively, without any recourse to logical thought or even a spoken word, she grasped who he was and why he had come— Lang Frazer, her father's partner. Equally strong came the notion that it was her destiny to have this man feel contempt for her. The sight of him, so dark and authoritative, the easy elegance of his beautiful clothes, filled her with the greatest foreboding so that it took actual courage for her to go forward and speak his name.

'Mr. Frazer?'

'Natalie.'

If she had expected to catch him off guard, he was no more surprised by her perception than she was, as though it was totally believable she should know him at once. He at least could see the cherished elfin child in the woman, for Drew still kept a tattered photograph of her in his wallet. She did not want to give him her hand, nor make any contact with him at all. His lean dark hardness and the imperious set of his head made him very different from any other man she had met, but good manners were as powerful a protection as anything else.

It seemed like the most momentous greeting of her life, her narrow hand in his. He had very lean, clever hands and she drew away from him quickly, her thick black lashes sweeping her cheekbones, veiling her eyes from him as all the painful old memories came surging back. This was Britt's cousin. She must never forget that. Besides, she had learned a great deal in these few years even though, now, it seemed a frail armour. She was standing gracefully, lifting her small face to him if only for a moment. 'I imagine you have something to say to me, Mr. Frazer, and you've certainly come a long way. Please come in. I have a dinner appointment, but I have a little time to spare.'

Almost for a moment he imagined he caught sight of a great sadness in her. Beautiful eyes, they always made one a part of it all. As soft and as grey as a mist shimmering with near tears, one of her deceptive little tricks. He made a little gesture with his hand, almost visibly rejecting her. 'Thank you,' he said curtly, irritated by her reference to a dinner engagement as though it could be important.

'This way, then!' Try as she did, she couldn't keep the throb out of her voice, hunting up the key to the stained timber door that led to the secluded little courtyard entry to the town house Grandfather Sabien's money had bought for her. He walked in silence beside her with no softening in his expression even though the tiny garden with its Japanese maple and its exquisite double flowering azaleas in their glazed Chinese pots presented a picture of the most beautiful tranquillity. As serene as the girl herself, he thought, and labelled her an accomplished actress. She had been very skilful as well with the whole arrangement, the plantings, the tiny white marble chips and irregular stepping stones, the small water garden with its timber surround.

Inside the small two-story unit, he could see at one glance that she had inherited her father's immense flair, a decorating style that was at once elegant and imaginative. It was said that to understand all was to forgive all, but he couldn't understand this girl at all. As an architect he had long since arrived at the conclusion the home and its interior decoration was an extension of self, in his own case a very good indication of what sort of client he could expect to have, yet he would have accepted Natalie Calvert as a client at once. She had solved all the usual dilemmas associated with transforming a basically boxlike structure brilliantly. It did not surprise him, not with her background, but it was a further piece of a puzzle that wouldn't fit. His burning blue scrutiny moved across the highly individual room appraising and appreciating despite himself. If he hadn't all the evidence he needed to the contrary he would have said Natalie Calvert was his own kind of woman, should such a woman exist. It was quite impossible at this stage to fathom what made her tick.

'Please sit down,' she said almost appealingly, dismayed by his height and his autocratic dark head.

Her voice like the rest of her appealed to his senses and he knew she was almost forcing herself to be pleasant. She sounded no more than a melancholy child and he almost groaned aloud with frustration or something equally dreary. How could she sound like that unless she had changed a great deal? She had been very young after all. What, seventeen, eighteen? She would be about twenty-three now with her thick black hair in a pageboy sliding across her impeccable white skin. She was sitting opposite him on a lovely old Victorian sofa upholstered in a Wedgwood blue velvet, on her face a rather frightened expression seeing the bitterness about his eyes and his mouth. His was a hard, handsome face, darkly austere, with a mastery few women would not recognise. Was it his intention to probe callously all the old wounds? He flickered a glance over her face and she felt the blue burning hostility. So distressing, and she had suffered enough. She slumped a little as though the burden of his contempt was too great a burden for her slender back. There was something about her that made him angry and uneasy at once and she knew

11

it would be difficult for him to treat her gently. Now, or in the future. It made her breathless just to have his glance touch her face and she moved a little fretfully calling attention to the slight trembling in her hands, sick with the sensation that what was about to happen had happened before.

'You've come about my father?'

'Of course!' Tension and involvement was crackling about them. 'You realise he's a very sick man?'

'I do,' she said quietly, 'and I'm more sorry than I can say.'

'At least there's room in your heart for a little compassion,' he said in a cool, cutting voice, as though he found the coldness of his own tone necessary. 'You never answered his letter. Why?'

'One letter in so many years, Mr. Frazer? Actually, I did answer it.'

'It never turned up!'

'*No*.' She gave an eloquent defeated little shrug. 'Britt's countless betrayals are something I've known about for a long time.' At the mention of his cousin's name, his eyes flared instantly into blue flame, but she tried to avoid their brilliant blue trap. 'I realise Britt is your cousin, but perhaps you don't know her as well as you think?'

'I know possessiveness flourishes in women,' he interrupted with hard mockery, 'but whatever the impasse between you and Britt, it's your father I'm concerned about. I happen to care what becomes of him. He's a brilliant architect and my good friend. When I returned from abroad five years ago he took me on instantly when quite a few of the big boys

12

were wary of my ideas. Your father had confidence in me and my so-called highly individual style and together we've done extremely well by anyone's standards. At the time of his stroke we simply couldn't handle the commissions that were pouring in—but that's beside the point. Today he's confined to a wheelchair with a recovery rate far slower than any of us anticipated. The stroke mercifully wasn't all that severe, yet his doctors, all of us, are full of anxiety for him. My own belief is he is wasting away with some kind of imagined remorse. About *you*. You know what kind of a man your father is, he still loves you and badly wants you home again.'

'*Still* loves me, Mr. Frazer,' she said with delicate irony. 'Why should he not love me? Does a parent stop loving a child or a child a parent? I don't think so. I can still feel very close to my father from thousands of miles away. The kind of relationship we had can never be entirely severed, not even with Britt to come between us. I can't deny that my father wounded me deeply and easily, simply because he is my father, but it's not he who is keeping me from his side. I can never go back to Maccalla with Britt there. She hates me, and all the good will in the world, on *my* side, and I admit I have none towards Britt, will ever change that. You see, Mr. Frazer, nothing changes and nothing can be forgotten. While you were making such a name for yourself overseas, your cousin Britt was forcing me out of my home. If I return to Maccalla the same old complications will start up again.'

'There will be no complications!' he said curtly.

'Ones you could never understand,' she cut him off with faint, desperate urgency, looking, of all things, endangered. Was it possible her face betrayed the real feelings that lay beneath the surface? Grey eyes caught the light—that was it, he thought with intense irritation. Many a man would be duped with that enchanting face. She was looking straight at him like some small bewildered flower, a sense of injustice weighing heavily on her delicate, straight shoulders. For an instant so strong was her look of her father, the same elegant bone structure, that his expression softened.

She recognised it at once and leaned towards him, speaking in a gentle, tranced tone: 'You can't mean to condemn me for ever and ever?'

'It's true I'm showing less tolerance towards you than anyone else I can recall, and I can't keep that up if we're to come to any workable arrangement. The way things are now I'm in and out of Maccalla nearly every day of my life. It would be impossible for us to avoid one another. You're too young to condemn and condemn, and I'm not the man to fight so fragile an enemy in any case. Whether we like it or not, the facts speak for themselves. Britt has never borne a child, and this is at the core of all her hidden pressures and resentments. To be fair to her she has never spoken of you unkindly, rather she steers more towards the theory you were excessively indulged as a child and not entirely to blame for your behaviour. Britt's story can't be shaken or denied, and perhaps this weighs heavily on your own conscience. She lost her baby, and with it the ability to have another child. Your father, much as he loves you, would dearly have loved a son. There's the business, and of course Maccalla. Britt blames you for her accident and so did your father, though Drew and I have never spoken of it. If you come back with me now, you have the opportunity to repay any harm you might have done. Make amends if you like. It's not often given to all of us.'

Her head jerked back sharply as if he had struck her and the white skin whitened still further. 'You've got your homework all wrong, Mr. Frazer!' she hurled at him, her luminous eyes for once flying storm clouds. 'I've nothing to make amends for! At the beginning there may have been some element of doubt, but I've long since come to the conclusion that there *was* no baby. Britt didn't want a baby at all. She would never share my father with anyone— not her own child, and certainly not another woman's. You simply don't know Britt, though I suppose she introduced you to my father and got you your job, whatever your undoubted gifts. Britt was and must still be tenacious in her power over my father. She mistrusted even his own secretary— but I suppose you don't know that. She had her fired anyway. My grandmother knew Britt at once and Britt took good care to keep out of Grand'-mère's way, but she didn't live long enough to help me. I had no one at the time of my father's remarriage and Britt fully exploited my vulnerability. It was fairly simple for her to find a way to force me out. My father was just a tool in the hands of a ruthless woman.

'Britt is capable of anything to achieve her own

ends. She has no moral sense, no set of rules to go by. I can see by your face that you're very angry, but you're going to hear me out. My father didn't believe in me enough to do that. He allowed himself to be tricked by a strong, possessive woman. I've gone over and over it these past years and there's more than enough room in my heart to forgive my father for his lack of faith in me. He simply had no experience of a woman like Britt. My mother was so very, very different. We never lied in our house before Britt came.'

'Consider that it's not uncommon either for serious conflict in a household when a parent remarries,' he said in a hard, matter-of-fact voice. 'Your life must have altered considerably. From all accounts you were reared like a princess. Lady Sabien, I have heard, worshipped you, and she was, of course, your maternal grandmother. It would be understandable perhaps if she felt some faint hostility towards my cousin, replacing her own daughter as it were, with Britt providing an heir for Maccalla, which is as we all know a very beautiful house and one of our finest examples of Colonial architecture. We can't forget to overlook Maccalla because I feel it plays quite a big part in the whole sad story. Britt has explained Lady Sabien to me.'

'How absurd!' said Natalie, her eyes sparkling with unshed tears. 'Britt to explain my grandmother? My grandmother was very well known in Adelaide, Mr. Frazer. She didn't need anyone to explain her. Certainly she disliked Britt, and she had excellent judgment. Far better than mine. Or yours,' she said hardily. 'I can see you've taken

Britt's every word as literally true.'

'Let us say, rather, I accept the word of my friend, who is also your father.'

With one stroke he seemed to have cut the ground from under her feet so that she lay back against the velvet sofa looking fragile enough to be breakable. Positively he looked away from her. Her face had a haunting fascination for him and he drove himself to focus on an interesting and unusual abstract painting that made quite a contribution to the room. His dark, handsome face with its trace of coldness and disdain wore a saturnine expression, his eyes were brilliantly sceptical. Every instinct warned him to be wary of her. With a face like that she could fool the beholder into believing anything she liked.

Her voice filled the silence, very soft and composed. 'You don't like women, do you, Mr. Frazer?'

He turned back to regard her, his mouth touched with satire. 'I know they're prone to obsessions.'

'More so than men? I expected my story to conflict utterly with Britt's, but I cannot accept that my father hasn't come to see Britt as she really is.'

'Britt is heading for a breakdown,' he said, and his mouth thinned.

'I expect she is if she thinks *I'm* coming back again. I won't be nearly so manoeuvrable this time.'

'It seems to me you're deliberately anticipating trouble.'

'I'm not such a fool as to expect to avoid it. I'll say no more about Britt's mental make-up. You won't listen. Once I would have over-defended myself passionately. I did to my father and he wrenched himself away from me. I'll never forget the expression in his eyes—the anger and the pain and the condemnation. I yielded to that. My father was very much in love with Britt—infatuated, my grandmother called it. My father had a clear choice and he chose to believe Britt. For my own part, I'm convinced there *was* no baby, and I swear I never pushed Britt down the staircase. She fell, but I never touched her. Whether she tripped or she threw herself I don't know—I was far too upset at the time to be a very accurate witness. She was hysterical, she hated me, and she said I pushed her, filled with jealousy and resentment over the coming baby. That my father could ever have believed that for one moment was at the time more than I could bear. Now I don't really care.'

'Don't sound so bitter!' he said, dismayed by her curious fragility.

'I've been on my own a long time, Mr. Frazer, and I'm not bitter at all. If you can't see that, you can't see anything. I've simply been denied my father and my home. You're quite right in thinking I loved Maccalla. It's quite possible to have a love affair with a house. You should know that, but there's nothing I can do about lost time. Perhaps I'm a little bitter about that. Even now my life is running through my fingers. Perhaps my father is dying? Perhaps Britt has reformed but still caught in a web of her own making. I don't know. I've been five years away from Maccalla—years full of tears and laughter, the odd day when I soar off into space with optimism and think everything will come right again, the other days when I could pine away with the sheer pain of rejection. Do you think I enjoy my modest surroundings after Maccalla? But I never want to find myself in Britt's Laocoön coils again. I always found her, from the day they arrived back from Europe, just as affable as a rattlesnake, a little mad in her obsession to have my father to herself. And the house. She covets Maccalla, you know.'

'So do a lot of people. You included,' he said.

'Not *covet*, Mr. Frazer, entirely the wrong word. I love Maccalla. I was born there. So was my father and his father before him. My great-grandfather built it, one of the finest architects of his day. Maccalla has a distinct personality. It welcomed everyone before Britt came. If Britt caused my father to reject me I believe the house will reject her.'

'That's stupid, morbid talk,' he said sharply. 'If you could see Britt as she is now you would feel for her.'

'You obviously do!'

'Of course I do! She's family, after all.'

'And a very attractive woman. Britt was always very clever with men, but she had little or no time for her own sex.'

'A trait you both share from the sounds of it,' he said, rather harshly, cynicism touching his clearly defined mouth.

'Yes, it could sound like that,' she said gravely, her smoke-coloured eyes veiled from him, 'but I never asked you to come here, Mr. Frazer. I've asked nothing of anyone. You're here on your own invitation with Britt's influence apparent!'

He stood up with lithe, uncoiled strength, his

hair-trigger alertness almost making her want to defend herself. 'My dear child!' he said forcibly, towering above her, 'allow me to set you straight about one thing at least. Britt had no idea I intended coming after you. Someone had to appeal to you, and it's blatantly obvious you've hardened your heart against Britt and your father. Britt mistrusts your temperament as much as you apparently mistrust hers, but she is far more mature in her appraisal of the situation than you are. You say my cousin hates you. It would be difficult indeed for me to accept the validity of that. She speaks of you with understanding and regret. She feels she failed you at a time when she was preoccupied with her own emotional upheaval. You insisted on seeing her as the proverbial wicked stepmother when she was merely a woman very much in love with her husband. That you were jealous and resentful of her is the classic situation, especially with an only child, and a capricious, wilful child at that. Britt claims she could never reach you as hard as she tried and your grandmother influenced you strongly against her. Why, she wrote to you many times in that first year before you moved North and she lost trace of you.'

'Britt never wrote to me,' she said wearily as though reciting a very difficult lesson. 'Neither did my father, but I always sent him a gift on his birthday and Father's Day and a week before Christmas. Nothing he ever did could make me forsake that kind of gesture. What my mother would have expected of me. My father didn't force me out of my home, for all he wounded me deeply—Britt did that. She made it impossible for me to remain. I would say too, she has always known where I lived. Britt is that kind of woman. She has to know everything.'

His eyes moved over her face with a kind of helpless frustration, as though she was inciting the sharpest emotions. 'That's simply not true, Natalie,' he said, his dark, high-cheekboned face intent on her. 'I've had to go to endless trouble myself trying to locate you. Do you really think Britt would put me through all that at a time when I could ill afford a misspent hour, let alone watch your father wasting away for want of a word from you? I tell you, you stubborn little girl, Britt loves your father. I've never heard anyone but you say anything different. She's devoted to him, while you, for such a young creature, are being remarkably cruel in a way only a woman knows, withholding her affection. Britt has said nothing to me that suggests she would deny you a welcome. All she wants is a responsible attitude from you and a little co-operation. It's up to you to face the truth!'

'What *is* the truth, Mr. Frazer? What really constitutes this truth of yours? The things that are said or the things that are never said. I will never live down all your cousin has said about me without contending with the things she has silently implied. You see, I don't think she loves my father at all. Not as my mother loved him, selflessly. Britt would hurt my father just to keep him all to herself and now I see I'm speaking of things you don't wish to hear.'

'You're right about that!' he said firmly. 'I want

21

no part of this at all, but the fact remains I'm very much involved. I'm your father's friend and his business partner. Britt is my cousin. You seem to be the catalyst among us. Because of you, and how you respond, so much depends.'

'Ironical to think you may turn out to be my unwilling champion,' she said strangely. 'You're a man completely sure of himself, sure of your gifts. Yet I sense that for all I apparently anger and irritate you, you're not entirely sure of *me*. Despite what Britt has said. It's all I can legitimately hope for if I return to Maccalla.'

'Not if, Natalie, *when*. As I see it, there's no other course open to you. You can and will make this gesture.'

A pulse was beating at the base of her throat and she pressed a hand to it instinctively. 'Even the way you use my name is a massive censure.'

He stood in front of her, very tall, very dark, an unutterably remote stranger. 'You're too sensitive!'

'Now that's an odd thing,' she said, her eyes shimmering, 'that couldn't have been your impression before you met me.'

His brilliant eyes moved over her face, her black hair that fell in a soft cascade against the side of her cheek. 'I would say you have the ability to suggest a lot of things. Whether it's right or not I have no means of telling and I don't intend to debate it over now.' He thrust his hand deep into his pocket and turned towards the abstract painting on the far wall. 'I like that.'

'The only thing about me you do like!' she snapped.

'You painted it?'

'You seem surprised, Mr. Frazer. I'm obviously a puzzle to you, and you take puzzles very seriously.' She had moved to his side, looking up at him. 'Why do you want to hurt me?'

'I don't want to hurt you. I just want to break you down a little for your own good.'

'You could be terribly wrong.'

'Five years ago, Natalie, you were what, seventeen? It might have happened in another lifetime. Whatever way we suffer we're supposed to learn something from it.'

She lowered her finely wrought face and her eyes misted over. He understood what the gesture meant and he lifted her chin, tilting her face back to him. 'The one thing I can't abide is a weeping woman.'

'Perhaps you'd better go, then. I want you to.'

'I won't go without your promise.'

'I have no choice about it,' she said. 'I'll come to Maccalla to see my father, and I want you to remember you brought me there.' His closeness was uncanny and she wanted to resist and resist him, afraid she was encountering some new dangerous force, to be moved relentlessly any way he wanted. 'I remember Maccalla the way it was and I had to escape. It will be the same again.'

He would have liked to deny it, but she was very serious, staring straight ahead, and he dropped his hand. 'Never the same again, Natalie. Your father is a sick man and Britt is in a pitiable state. When can you come? I must go back myself in the morning.'

'A week at the most,' she said, and turned her

head away, still distressed.

'A week may be **too** long.'

'All right, then, **in the** morning,' she said, her eyes widening and flying to him, 'but you'd better call for me because I may change my mind—you see, I know this trip is ill advised.'

'How can it be when it's helping your father?' His eyes, blue and challenging, held hers. 'Your father needs you.'

'He didn't need me before. You mentioned remorse. If my father is feeling remorseful, perhaps he has a few things to be remorseful about. The absence of love can be just as terrible as its loss. I've been absent from my father's love for a long time now. Britt is my enemy, a natural enemy if you like —and don't look so scornful, Mr. Frazer, though it's a look that suits you well. Britt makes plans, calculated to the last second, with never a move misjudged.' She could see his mind automatically rejecting her statements as though he was a man long immune to a woman's dramatics.

'There's no satisfaction in self-pity, Natalie.'

'And there's no mistaking hate when you see it,' she cried out, unrepentant. 'It's in the eyes if no other place.'

For answer he pushed her gently back into an armchair, courteously restrained, but she felt the dark metalled anger in him. 'If we're going to have a slanging match we might as well sit down again. Most of us object to a bit of honesty when it doesn't reflect too well on ourselves. Listen to me, Natalie. Britt, too, has many friends, none of whom would recognise her from your description.'

'My *extravagances*,' she said a little bitterly, recognising that he was calling up some excitement in her. 'One must fall into a certain category to incite her jealous hostility. Men can be only admirers.'

'She has made your father a good wife,' he pointed out with weary patience. 'She's an excellent hostess for Maccalla—or she was before Drew's stroke. Now everything has changed. Britt too. She's living on her nerves and I'm worried about her. The effect of Drew's stroke on her has been devastating. When you see her you'll realise she's on the verge of a nervous breakdown.'

'Then it's likely I might push her right over the edge! Have you thought of that, Mr. Frazer? When you ring Britt to tell her you've located me and intend bringing me back to Maccalla you'd better tell her in the next breath I'll be there for about a week only. A longer period might drive her demented.'

'Don't you think you're becoming a little tedious about Britt?'

'Don't you think you're asking a great deal of me? Even allowing for the fact Britt is your cousin and a very clever woman, it's Britt who is living in my home, not me.'

'Then I'm right in thinking Maccalla plays a big part in all your corroding resentments.' There was a flash of steel in the blue brilliance of his eyes and she looked away from them.

'I can't and won't listen to any more!' she exclaimed, with a frantic little gesture, crossing her hands in front of her face and bowing her head into them for protection. 'It took real courage for me to speak to you this afternoon and it's going to take a great deal more to go back to Maccalla, but I'll do as you ask because I *do* love my father. I'll make my peace with him if that's what he wants, assure him I'm quite happy in my own way of life and able to look after myself.'

'And quite well, Natalie,' he said, drawing her hands from her face. 'You call your surroundings modest, but the average girl would never agree with you. There are a few really good pieces in this room.'

'My grandmother's.'

'Of course. You figured very largely in Lady Sabien's will.'

He still held her hands loosely and she drew them away sharply as though his touch hurt her. 'I don't think that's altogether your business, Mr. Frazer.'

'Which, of course, it isn't!' he agreed dryly, his eyes on all that furious young pride, every movement of her body suggesting he was injuring her. In another sphere she could make a marvellous actress. A star performer, very beautiful, and her voice had quality too. 'It's just that you tend to sound as if you were plucked from the nest without a feather to fly with, to freeze in a garret.'

'Do I sound like that?' she asked, her composure returning, her softly shimmering eyes sweeping up to his face, full of a wry humour. 'One can't freeze in Queensland. At the same time I think *you* sound excessively high-handed, now we're both being so devastatingly honest.'

'Obviously we act as counter-irritants, Natalie, but that doesn't really matter. I've accomplished what I intended. To take you back to Maccalla

26

where you will give your father a new lease of life.'

'Or I'll have you to answer to, is that it? I distinctly detected a threat there. Not necessary, believe me.' For a moment she was very quiet, withdrawn, then she said: 'Now I've a good many phone calls to make. Fortunately I'm almost freelance these days.'

'Freelance what, Natalie?'

'Didn't you find out?' she challenged him, and quickly on impulse got up and moved away from him. 'I mentioned it in the letter to my father that never arrived. As well, in the usual way, I put my address on top. I'm in interior design, Mr. Frazer. One of these days when I have more experience I'm hoping to open my own business.' She swung about and faced him, her silk skirt swirling gracefully. 'They tell me I've a certain flair.'

'Yes.' He flickered a glance over her and she could feel her heart begin to beat rapidly. There was something sensual in his face as well as ascetic, just as there was a trace of protectiveness under all that hard cynicism. She might never like him or feel comfortable with him, but she could trust him to be scrupulously fair once he knew the true facts. His blazing blue eyes made a quick circuit of the room, professionally appraising. 'Perhaps your father can put up some capital?'

'I still have Grandfather Sabien's money, as you were good enough to point out,' she said with her own sweetly piercing little irony. 'The death duties were enormous. I'm by no means an heiress and there were all Grand'mère's pet charities and a big legacy to cancer research—my mother had a rare bone cancer. My life would have been very different had she lived.'

'There's no denying that!' he said with his first flash of compassion. 'Losing your mother, then your grandmother within a few years must have affected you deeply. Perhaps all this hatred and antagonism of Britt's you speak about, this way you have of seeing her as some malignant personal enemy, is the result of your own traumatic experiences?'

'I still had my father,' she said quietly. 'We had one another!'

'That couldn't continue indefinitely, Natalie. Apart from the fact that your father found himself a widower early in life, you were bound to marry and make a home of your own. Drew was, and is, when we get him well again, a handsome, dynamic man with everything to live for. It was only to be expected he would remarry.'

'Perhaps, but none of us expected Britt. Having Father and Maccalla to herself became a kind of religion, in fact it's hard to say which was the bigger fantasy, my father or Maccalla,' Natalie explained. 'She was obsessed with both. All I know is it was a bewildering experience watching Britt's transformation after she married Father. She was quite charming to me up until then. Britt is a very strange woman, full of unfathomable feelings. Now you're asking me to set a spark to the flame again. The years must have given Britt an even stronger grip on my father and our home, yet now you're asking me to love her like a sister. It can't be done. She's only twelve years older than I am. If I was too simple for her once, I'll never be again. Besides,

Mr. Frazer, I'm depending on you to be amazingly watchful, even if only to prove yourself right and me wrong. One thing no one can take from me is a sense of my own integrity. You've only seen Britt softly weeping or smiling. I've seen her snarling in a white-hot rage.'

'Good God, child!' he said with fresh urgency. 'No one is entirely black or entirely white but rather a variety of colours. I get no picture of Britt as a Lady Macbeth at all. She's a cultivated, attractive woman, devoted to her husband. These wild stories of yours try me too far. Without your being aware of it perhaps it's an unhappy lack in yourself, a lack of generosity towards a woman other than your mother whom your father can love. If so, you should be ashamed of yourself.'

'The one thing I assuredly don't suffer from is shame,' she said vibrantly, her searching, glowing grey eyes intent on his face, her young, slender body tautened like a bowstring. 'Britt's ghost still troubles my nightmares, curiously cold and chilling. Don't blame me if I can't believe in some miraculous change.'

Lang Frazer drew an audible breath and his white teeth snapped. 'You're either a superb actress or a child deeply wronged. What is it you want of me?'

'Protect me,' she said oddly, and fell silent, a pulse beating rapidly in her white throat.

He put his hands on her shoulders and turned her fully towards the soft radiance of late afternoon sunlight. 'Wronged or not, Natalie,' he said softly, 'I'm going to knock a few of these big chips from

29

your shoulders. You can't continue to think as you do, you may permanently tilt your personality. Britt *can't* be as bad as you say. Perhaps you've extravagantly embroidered your memory. Britt told me she felt your relationship was poisoned from the beginning with outside influences.' He felt her instant, instinctive withdrawal, but he still held her with his lean, strong hands.

'If you're referring to my grandmother—?'

'Calm down, child!' He could feel the trembling right through her. 'Your grandmother had the reputation of being rather grandly eccentric!'

'If you mean she drank champagne for breakfast so would I if I had my own vineyard. My grandmother was a warm and wonderful woman, very clear and direct. There was no room in her life for paltry intrigue and venomous little vendettas. She had a marvellous, sweeping, romantic nature. Surely you've heard that?'

For a second only a flash of amused communication passed between them. 'As a matter of fact, I have! Yet your grandmother never came to Britt and your father's wedding?'

'No. She said she didn't like parties any more, even interesting ones. She simply radiated health and vitality up until my mother died, then she seemed to grow old overnight. What she felt for Britt was not so much dislike as foreboding, the afterwards.'

'She influenced you strongly, you will admit that?'

'It would be infamous to deny it, but if you think she filled my head with melodramatic and gloomy predictions, she did not!'

'Yet she never saw Britt as mistress of Maccalla?'

'I doubt if she ever saw anyone else but my mother as that. It was a matter of temperament. My grandmother was a grande dame, very family-minded. I've even known people to tremble at her very word, but she was gentle underneath and still beautiful at eighty-two.'

'If she influenced you unwisely, Natalie, it was understandable. Your mother was her only child and your grandmother's life centred around both of you.'

'Grand'mère had nothing to do with it,' she said tiredly, astonished by the impulse she had to just rest her head against him. 'The grim fact is that I never want to lay eyes on Britt again. There's no security for me with her about.'

He said nothing, but she could feel the baffled anger in him.

'Britt just has to be the queen bee and I don't ever want to fall into her web again. What she did to me could have been tragic. The only thing that saved me was the feeling that somehow her allegations were groundless.'

'Would a woman lie about a thing like that?' He tilted her face up, his hand hard on her chin.

'About what?' she whispered, a little frightened of him.

'About the baby!' he said with mingled pity and anger. 'As Britt told it to me she desperately wanted to give your father the son he longed for.'

'While my mother was alive my father seemed perfectly happy with *me*!' said Natalie, and the tears came into her eyes. 'Perhaps Father did want a son, but then I would have loved a small brother. You obviously haven't considered that. Britt's supposed desperation for a child isn't consistent with my view of her temperament. She detested to put on a single ounce of weight—in fact she was fanatical with her diet regime. But that's all in the past, yesterday. For five long years I've been living in another land; now you want me to go back. I don't think it can be done, and if it can, not without help!'

For an instant the memory of the grief she had felt at her father's perjured love for her flashed across her face. She could, if she returned to Maccalla, be betrayed again. Britt's dupe, with the mocking lost cry of a child between them. Love was a wilderness and obsessive love the greatest jungle of all. Suddenly it was unbearable to stay within range of Britt's cousin and defender. He could never have any virtue in her eyes, a glimmer of gold overlaying his skin so that it seemed in its contemptuous remoteness to be a dark copper mask, with an idol's cold and glittering sapphire eyes.

So complete was her despair he was drawn by its vibrations. What did she think he was threatening —treachery?

'Don't look so harried,' he said curtly, cursing the fact that his own feelings and interests were involved. 'I promise you no one is going to hurt you.'

'And if they do, it will be *your* fault!' She whirled on him with a swift grace and certainty, her silky black hair flying forward to caress her white cheek. 'You see this return to Maccalla as my soul's salvation,' she said passionately.

'I *see* it,' he bit out, triumphing over her with his height and authority, 'as this: if you don't come back and anything should happen to your father, you may be committing yourself to a lifetime of intolerable regret.' He spoke forcibly and had the satisfaction of seeing her wide, black-lashed grey eyes waver, then fall. He didn't care to analyse it, but the fact was being driven home on him, he would have liked to shake her until all her elegant bones rattled, such was her effect on him. She had, he realised, an aura of femininity to its highest degree. No opulent thing but something most delicately and subtly conveyed, a kind of witchcraft against which he had to be wary. Everything about her was at odds with all his accumulated data, but then she could have a great talent for acting. Instead of sullen, stubborn resentment, here was this lovely, bitterly wounded young face. It didn't make sense and neither did he, and his eyes went glittery with self-mockery.

Natalie was standing there almost transfixed, with all the sweet vitality of the afternoon drained out of her, a kitten without a home and an aching desire to rest. Lang's white teeth snapped with irritation. Her defencelessness alone should have tempered this strange sexual antagonism he had for her, but it didn't. It was feeding it. Whatever she was and whatever he believed her to be, he couldn't deny he very much wanted to keep her within sight.

'Perhaps as you're coming with me in the morning you might cancel your dinner appointment,' he suggested sardonically.

33

There was a communication of tension between them that went far beyond his actual words. 'I can't,' she said gently. 'Adrian is also my boss.'

'Of course.' His blue eyes flamed and the contempt was back on his face again. 'If it's all right with you, I'd like to take the first flight in the morning. Eight-fifty. I've taken the liberty of booking your ticket.'

Defiance dawned in her misty grey eyes. 'You're very sure of yourself, Mr. Frazer.'

His brilliant glance flickered over her with that inexplicable little clash of hostilities. 'It won't hurt you, Natalie, to be managed. In that way you'll never mix me up with anyone else.'

'I'll never do that!' she observed wryly. They were, she knew, moving into a new sphere, a dangerous, shivery excitement that could destroy all her hard-won peace.

He moved so abruptly she retreated a step herself, colour flaring along her cheekbones as she caught the brilliant irony in his eyes, the amused acceptance that she thought herself trapped.

'I'll call for you, shall I?' he asked, his voice silky with satire and something else she couldn't define and was really afraid to.

'Thank you.' She walked to the door with him, realising how great were the differences between them, but pride forbade her to cry out her reluctance to go with him. For her father's sake she had to sacrifice herself, and that was how she saw it—a sacrifice. If it was truly said that a tiger could never change his stripes, neither then could a tigress.

CHAPTER TWO

Britt Calvert paced rhythmically around the quiet opulence of her bedroom as though she sought escape from some unbearable prison. Nothing could calm the tossing turbulence of her mind—Pills, drink, nothing. Night was the worst, when once she had loved it. The gay social life, the dinner parties, the entertaining, she the gracious hostess, Drew at her side, drawing the envy of scores of their women friends, beautiful Maccalla abloom with flowers and lights, cars parked six deep in the drive.... Her mouth twitched with self-pity, her mind even now refusing to accept the fact that it was all over. It was her sleek pampered body that fought the long hours of crippling inactivity, the futile black hours of raging against gods who had smiled on her only to turn malicious.

What could she salvage from the wreck of her life if not Maccalla? The passion she had felt for Drew that had once burned so brightly had razed itself out. His illness appalled her; all illness did. It took an enormous effort of will to go near him at all. She shuddered in horror, her revulsion pathological, and her long golden eyes flickered. They could all of them, Lang, the doctors, that fool of a nurse Janet Clark, talk hopefully of Drew's recovery. *She* knew he would never recover. His speech that had been affected was now restored to him, but his lean strong body was marred for ever. He would never be the same man again, her lover. With only the empty shell of a marriage what else was left to her but Maccalla? Her eyes were fathomless in her white face. No one, it could be said, knew Britt, and hers was no happy soul for all it was camouflaged by her physical attributes. Just as the reddish gold tigress running smooth and purposeful through the jungle could appear almost grey against her background, so could Britt take on the colour of her surroundings, adapting herself to every circumstance with unerring instinct, working always towards her own ends. Britt, too, like the tigress, could purr with satisfaction, and only when she felt herself threatened did the furies that drove her become apparent. That she felt threatened now was reflected in the blind frustration of her prowl, not so very different from that of a wild creature bound down to captivity.

Through the adjoining door, she could hear Drew in his sleep make a faint moaning sound, then a few incoherent words fell from his lips like an agony of regret. Britt swished across the room, her silk robe dragging on the carpet in a cold panic as she closed the door. She couldn't bear much more of it. Today had been a bad day for all of them. A good day for losers—but she hadn't lost yet. There was still Maccalla, a strikingly beautiful house by anyone's standards, somehow managing to be both grand and romantic. The ownership of it was of vital importance to her. If she lost Maccalla now it would seem as if she had lost everything. Almost as if she had never been Mrs. Andrew Calvert, established in a superlative way of life with wealth and position and an old family name.

She wasn't like Lang, whose brilliance lifted him above everyone else. It was because of Drew and Maccalla that her life had taken on a shape and a form. If she were to lose Drew she could never lose the magnificent status symbol that was the house. She was intensely possessive of it, though there was never a time that she had felt secure in it, more like a trespasser with the house at war with her. Maccalla was a prize she constantly feared would be snatched from her, and there was only one. *One* face fixed in her mind, and her hatred and fear was a physical thing, the throbbing arrowheads of tension that could not be denied—and for Lang to bring her here! The very thought filled her with cold fury. Would she never be rid of the girl? Her triumph had not been complete. What had been so simply achieved before might be difficult again. After five years that pearly innocence and mute young pride would no longer exist. Time had a way of changing everything, yet the past was never dead. Her memories of the young Natalie had never faded.

Tonight of all nights Britt could not exorcise her devils. They were like great birds swooping for her. She would have a few neat whiskies to ease some of her tensions, then she would have to plan for the coming ordeal. It was some measure of encouragement that she had succeeded the last time. All that she had worked for, the peace and the beauty and security, she could never let slip through her fingers....

They came to Maccalla by way of a winding private road that led up to the leafy green folds of the foothills. The Calverts' place in the sun, an estate that had once encompassed twenty acres of parkland sold off in lots over the years until the property was reduced to a little over two acres of beautifully tended lawns and gardens, a camellia walk, a sunken rose garden, great banks of azaleas and rhododendrons with their showy orange and flame trusses breaking in waves up to twenty feet high, masses and masses of hydrangeas in the summertime and a wonderful bush house that housed all the exotic ferns and foliage plants and a wide selection of orchids, native, and the luminous beauties from all over the world.

Richard Calvert, later knighted by the Queen for his services to the Colony, purchased the land in the early 1800s barely six months after his arrival by ship from England. An architect by profession and a 'gentleman of substance,' the cottage where he lived while supervising the building of Maccalla and its outlying stables and coachhouse was still preserved in the grounds, serving as a charming little summer retreat and on occasions in Andrew Calvert's time as extra accommodation when the big house overflowed with guests. All the Calverts from first to last were marked by their love and gift for entertaining.

Maccalla was the epitome of the graceful style Richard Calvert had introduced into the Colony. From its vantage point on the western slopes of the ranges, it commanded a magnificent view over the city and the shimmering blue light of the Gulf of

St. Vincent. Colonial architecture at its very best, combining Regency classicism with the adaptation of wide, deep verandas and sparkling white shutters and jalousies so necessary for protection against the long, hot Australian summers. Maccalla emerged a large, elegant private mansion in harmony with its surroundings. Where once peacocks and tame emus used to roam there was now an emerald green ornamental lake with its great stands of iris and swans to sail across its mirror-smooth expanse.

Through the soaring line of the trees Natalie caught her first sight of the roof of Welsh slate, and the whole complicated nature of the position she was in overwhelmed her. She had a sensation of unreality, yet all her old memories came back at a rush. Freesias, the scent of creamy white freesias so strong and sweet, brought it all back. On just such a beautiful spring day with the white cherry blossom and the magnolias out she had left Maccalla. It had looked just the same then with the blue sky and the ranges for a backdrop and shimmering through the trees the gentle tranquillity of the lake. It would take a great effort not to dwell on the past, but she found herself remembering it vividly all the same. Maccalla had always affected her to an extreme degree—and now to turn the pendulum back!

'Maccalla never changes!' she said, trying hard not to become over-emotional. 'Honey-coloured sandstone and white cast-iron lace, a four-storey tower and a wonderful porte-cochère. When my mother was alive the house was never without some kind of social activity. She and Grand'mère had so many charities to look after. We had friends staying from all over the country and always one or other of Papa's relations over from England. I know Maccalla is beautiful,' she said ardently, 'yet I've never been able to describe it properly.'

'You're too close to it,' said Lang. 'Maccalla is a particularly happy combination of classic and romantic, a very personal kind of architecture and built with great skill. Most of our tradesmen came from England and they were trained at a time when English domestic architecture was at its best. Everywhere at Maccalla you'll find a uniformly excellent standard of workmanship. The house itself is imposing, yet it's very graceful, and of course money was never a consideration. Sir Richard, as we know, inherited a quite comfortable fortune and he built for the moneyed, educated class. It all helps.'

He glanced across at Natalie, her head slightly turned from him the sun cutting a path across the exquisite white of her skin. 'The building trade always reflects the economy. In your great-grandfather's day and especially after the Gold Rush of Bathhurst and Ballarat architecture was really booming—homes, hotels, halls, churches, city halls, offices, warehouses. People wanted all kinds of buildings, not only the powerful landed gentry but the new commerce. Some made fortunes on the goldfields and others made bigger fortunes catering to the diggers. A lot of our big business houses were founded then. Maccalla reflects an affluent society.'

'Would you want a house like that yourself?' she asked oddly, turning to look at him.

A smile broke over his mouth like a shower of

light, a sparkle of white against his deep tan. 'Not at all, Natalie. When the time comes, I'll build my own house. I have my own vision, not another man's. It's not yesterday either. It's today.'

'And my difficulty is I hanker after yesterday—is that what you're trying to say?'

'If I wanted to say something, Natalie, I *would*. I usually shun enigmatic statements.'

'Oh, I didn't know!' She smiled at him in turn and he glanced away from her. Her mouth alone would make her fortune, and his lean handsome face hardened cynically.

'I know you like to get people neatly boxed in, Mr. Frazer.'

'Not *boxed* in, Natalie, surely?' he said with the maddening reasonableness of an adult to a child. 'I'm a good architect, I hope.'

'You know you are. There wouldn't be much point in arguing that. I would think you always have very definite ideas about everything. *Everyone.*' She glanced at him speculatively and he returned her gaze, his blue eyes very brilliant. For a split second their eyes held and Natalie felt as though she had taken another giant step in the wrong direction.

'Are you begging me to reserve judgment on you, Natalie?'

'I am.'

In his shocking blue eyes was a mixture of amusement and self-mockery. 'You don't have to beg for anything, not with eyes like a sea mist and hair like black silk.'

For an instant so disturbing was his tone she

41

found it hard to speak her senses in a tempest. 'Was that a grudging admission, Mr. Frazer? You obviously think you have to be cruel to be kind.'

'It's considered sound psychology generally.' There was an odd blend of mockery and something she couldn't place in his tone. She swung her head away from him and her thick smooth hair danced like a black flame. This cool, uncaring man was raising vibrations deep within her, and the worst part was he knew it.

'Five years almost to the day since I walked out of here,' she said, and despite herself her eyes shone with tears. 'I know this is stupid of me, but I want you to pull up for a moment, near the lake. I want to see the swans—they'll calm me. As a child I used to walk over the little half moon bridge with the white cast-iron rails. The detailing is beautiful, the scrolls and motifs, the same as up at the house.'

'Yes, I know.'

Lang pulled off the gravel road and slid the car into a deep pocket of shade underneath a magnificent old gum. With the engine stilled it was very quiet with only the scent of the earth around them, the budding shrubs and trees and then the song of a bird like something symbolic seeping comfort to her sore heart. Across the gleaming silver-shot water eight white swans were gliding with two red-billed black swans for company and two more in the sunlit, reed-fringed shallows. Nothing it seemed could surpass them in beauty, their effortless serene sailing. As she watched their matchless progress, Natalie's expression grew tender and her sensitive mouth curved. She was calming herself with the beautiful scene that was offered to her. A lovely transparency of light drifted down through the leafy canopy of the tree, tingeing her grey eyes with a mysterious green. She looked a very young witch, but no less dangerous, Lang thought, his dark face thoughtful, seemingly intent on the swans but in reality waiting for her lovely low voice, as moving as it was undeniably moved by this place.

'My father used to call us his two swans, Mother and I,' she said, turning her body with fluid grace. 'There used to be a big heavy gold-framed portrait of us up at the house. *Nadia, Natalie.* Papa hung it above the fireplace in the drawing room. He commissioned it from a friend who is also a famous artist. You would know him if I told you his name. He always said it was one of his favourites— Mamma, like Grand'mère, silvery fair, myself at near ten, peering like some black-haired changeling over the linked semicircle of Mamma's pretty linked hands. My father swore he would never part with it. Is it there now?'

It was a battle to answer her without showing his own emotions. 'No, Natalie, it's not. I've never seen it.'

'I was almost certain of that before I asked,' she said, and stopped suddenly, catching her breath. 'Britt used to hate it.'

'God!' He drew in his breath sharply.

'Don't be angry. I'm just saying Britt will be my enemy until the last day of my life.'

'That must be the tenth time, Natalie. Britt's name is beginning to sound like an accompaniment.' Almost without his own volition he caught her narrow shoulders, drawing her towards him, either not knowing or caring that he was hurting her. 'You can be sure of one thing,' he said harshly. 'I'll allow nothing and no one to harm you.'

'Why would you seek to protect me?' she asked in a strange tone.

'I brought you here and you're Drew's daughter.'

'You'll save me despite myself?'

'Yes, if you want to put it like that.'

'Then I couldn't ask for anything better, could I?'

There was a hint of a tremble in her voice and Lang's punishing hold slackened. 'Natalie, it's time you got over a few of your notions,' he said very seriously.

'Sticks and stones!' she chanted off-key. 'You won't hurt me that way. I've come to see my father and beyond that I don't care to think. You *are* hurting my arms, though.'

'I'm sorry. How perfectly churlish of me.'

'I'm sorry too. I can't go on protesting my innocence of all the things you seem to have stacked up against me. Perhaps it was all my fault in a way.' She knew as she said it how it might sound, but she was too unnerved by her own jumbled emotions to change anything. She wanted him to trust her no matter what, but it was a tall order and his obvious interpretation of her meaning created an inevitable barrier between them. She would keep the memory of the swans and their serenity stored inside her. The thought lightened her expression and he glanced at her quickly. 'I'm just telling myself my

44

father is the only person really important and other people don't matter at all,' she explained. The old reminiscent bitterness could not be allowed to remain. Britt had always displayed extraordinary amounts of self-control when the occasion demanded it, why couldn't she?

His searing blue glance rained down on her face. 'Trust me,' she heard herself saying when she never meant to say it at all.

'That isn't going to be the easiest thing, I know.'

'No. I can see it will be difficult for me ever to reach you.'

'You're here to see your father, Natalie,' he pointed out. 'And I'll help you in every way I can. I think you're just panicking a little. Try to remember that Britt does love your father. You must give credit where credit is due.'

And that's it! Natalie thought, retiring into her greatest refuge of silence. Let him think what he liked. That women didn't need reasons for incompatibility. That it was impossible for two women to live happily under the one roof. That five years before she had been no more than a spiteful, vengeful adolescent trying to frustrate her well-meaning stepmother at every turn. That Britt would never allow anyone to frustrate her ambitions Lang Frazer might not be expected to know. He had never seen those gold blazing eyes and that wild passionate mouth, a greedy mouth. Somehow, Natalie thought, she would have to make this confrontation as painless as possible for her father's sake. With the best will in the world she couldn't see how Britt's attitude towards her would change.

45

Britt was unyielding; it was her very nature.

Natalie's mouth grew dry and her breathing a little uneven. What had really happened five years ago? Would anyone ever know? But the pattern could never be repeated. She was no longer an inexperienced girl. Even so, she was no match for Britt and she would be making a big mistake to think so.

'Natalie?' Lang Frazer turned his dark head abruptly. There was a strong dash of the autocrat about him, but he was a sensitive man and her distress was reaching him in tiny tumbled waves.

'I'm quite all right. A bit nervous, of course, and dreadfully anxious about my father—but please let's go on. When we come out of the cypress grove we'll have our first complete view of the house. Commanding attention to itself, Grand'mère used to say, but she loved it. How will I find my father?'

'Inexpressibly happy to have you home again,' he said simply. 'You belong together.' His eyes, the quicksilver blue of the sea, glinted over her. 'So don't go tearing yourself to pieces. The sight of you will be enough for him.'

'I hope so,' she sad fervently.

Blue eyes had a peculiarly magnetic quality, she thought, willing herself to look away from him, her own eyes grown brilliant with her heightened awareness. It would be the pinnacle of folly to allow herself to become emotionally involved with Lang Frazer. He was first and last Britt's cousin, and that should tell her something. He certainly took her part, but then Britt had always been very clever with men. She would have to display her own self-possession. This wasn't alien country, this was her own home, Maccalla, and it was welcoming her. She could tell.

They swept out of the cypress grove and she caught her breath, seeing everything with shattering clarity. It was twice as beautiful, the past and the present swelling and swirling together, shimmering like the waves of the sea. Maccalla was as much a part of the scene as the foothills were part of the ranges. The house and everything in it *was* the Calverts. Surely someone famous had once said: We shape our dwellings and afterwards our dwellings shape us. Natalie only knew her home was of great importance to her and it always would be. Maccalla was forever touched with splendour.

The blood tingled in her veins, giving her cheeks unaccustomed colour. The eyes sought and found all her favourite sanctuaries in the garden—the magnificent shade trees, the unexpected little gardens in the extensively landscaped grounds, the long beds of tulips and poppies, the daffodils massed around the white flowering cherry, Fuji Kofima, the scented star magnolias. In this golden spring, the azaleas seemed to have taken over, running in great drifts of snow white and all through the pinks down to the lake with its stands of iris and hyacinths and floating the lotus lilies of blue and ivory.

She looked towards the house and her throat tightened. It would be extremely difficult for her not to show the threatening tide of emotion. Five years it had been, yet it seemed like yesterday. She might be returning from a friend's party. But Lang Frazer wasn't a friend. He might not be her enemy

47

either, but she sensed the resistance in him as though he was deliberately keeping a tight rein on himself.

They were circling the drive now, drawing abreast of the house, and the raised formal gardens slipped into the cool shade of the porte-cochère, perfectly proportioned and decorated, an elegant shelter for the carriages of her great-grandfather's day. Somehow Natalie was out of the car, looking through the deeply recessed and carved front door into the white and gold of the entrance hall. The beautiful, glittering chandelier was still there, hanging from an ornate rose in the ceiling. A woman was coming down the graceful divided stairway, clutching the cedar handrail, her tawny hair bright against the gleaming dark panelling. The shock of the sight of her passed from Natalie's eyes to her brain.

'Natalie, Natalie, my dear. Welcome, welcome!'

For a moment Natalie thought she might faint. Only the familiar voice was the same. This wasn't Britt, a strong woman sure of her own strength, superbly groomed and at the peak of her physical condition. The ghost of the woman who had plagued Natalie so long was gliding down the staircase. Natalie stood as if hypnotised, unable to speak with the scent of the star magnolias floating in on the wind. Who was this thin bewildered woman, her nerves strung to a high pitch, her slanting gold eyes filled with a wild kind of grief? She looked a woman tearing herself to pieces with anguish over her husband. She looked ill.

Almost for a moment Natalie felt her heart going

out to her, then Britt was upon her, embracing her, and after the first shock Natalie found the embrace extraordinarily chilling. She couldn't cringe, yet she wanted to; her own nerves were drawn out perilously fine. Tangling with Britt was like going in at the deep end. Some women were elemental, and Natalie was convinced Britt was one of them. The thoughts that pass through one's mind! Should she say delighted to be back and add to this feeling of farce? Britt's skin was stretched taut across her high cheekbones, her full mouth working, such a pleading in her tawny eyes for co-operation, a willingness to forget the past. Natalie could have sworn she was sincere, only she knew well enough the expressions of helplessness Britt could assume when the circumstances required it. It was one thing to be prepared for an exchange of insults, but this? Britt was quite literally shaking and a tear trembled, then trickled down her sharply contoured cheek. Natalie stared at it in fascination.

'Don't let our memories of the past come between us!' Britt said in a husky, moved voice. She was still holding Natalie's hands and she must have felt Natalie's instinctive resistance, for she gently dropped them at once.

'No, of course not!' Natalie managed in a soft, polite voice, the only voice she could find. It was a sickening thought that perhaps her response to Britt's pleas might be proof of her own immaturity. It was impossibly presumptuous to set oneself up as a censor of human behaviour. Britt looked pathetic, so why should this most unworthy notion persist that all the old infighting could be revived again at

49

the drop of a hat? Two fighters in a ring: I've licked you before and I'll lick you again. Britt's very nature would make any kind of contest unequal.

Britt's eyes shone opaquely like yellow glass. She paused helplessly as though her worst fears were confirmed and there was no chance of Natalie's rehabilitation at all, then she turned and looked back at Lang Frazer, who had come silently into the entrance hall, standing well back and watching the two women with his piercing blue scrutiny.

'Lang, my dear!' Britt held out two hands and without a moment's hesitation, her cousin moved forward with the lithe grace that seemed to be characteristic of him and took them. The lines of strain around Britt's nose and mouth slackened perceptibly and she began to look more like herself. 'How good of you to bring Natalie back to us. You're much, *much* too good to us, my dear!'

'There's nothing I wouldn't do to get Drew well again,' he answered, a deep note of concern in his attractive, dark-timbred voice. 'You're thinner, Britt, and you can ill afford a weight loss.'

'Don't worry about me, darling. One of the penalties of loving too much, I suppose. I'm just as graceful to you as I can be. There can be no better cure than to be loved, to be surrounded by one's loved ones.'

Britt's mellifluous mezzo rang with the sweet sound of truth and Natalie had the dismal idea that she would be stuck with a guilt complex for the rest of her life. She was positively unnerved by this strange new gaunt woman with the crusading zeal in her eyes of a saint.

'Please, Natalie!' Britt was saying anxiously, stretching out a hand in the age-old gesture of appeal. 'When you see your father, try not to excite him. Oh, I know how he'll feel, you were always the apple of his eye, but my dear, if anything should happen to him ...!' She broke off, lacking the heart and the energy to go on, and Lang Frazer intervened, an excellent audience of one.

'Britt!'

'Don't worry, dearest!' she silenced him with a brave air. 'I'm quite all right. I only want what's best for my husband. It's all I have ever wanted. If it makes Drew happy to have Natalie here, that's what *I* want. Natalie will always have a welcome in my home.'

As a piece of acting it was superb, a masterpiece. The theatre had lost a great star. Certainly, Natalie thought, I should hang my head in shame or fling myself on the floor and howl for forgiveness if only I hadn't learned the hard way all Britt's little traits. If only I hadn't witnessed a better performance five years ago before I was banished to limbo! She stood stricken, hearing the nervous thud of her heart. It was a most peculiar sensation, being caught in a maze of deceit.

'Perhaps you should go up to your father now,' Lang Frazer suggested rather testily, for no other reason than that he wanted to get between Britt's unwinking gold stare and Natalie. She was standing with all the frozen elegance of a Japanese lady, her shining smooth hair swinging thick and black. She seemed to be offering no provocation at all, yet

51

wasn't her beauty the greatest provocation of all? Britt was an experienced woman, and this child ...? 'Now!' he repeated with the damnably odd compulsion on him to protect her, but from God knew what. His sombre dark face and his voice was fraught with his own tensions. He sounded incredibly arrogant and he saw the tears start to her lovely grey eyes. What else could he do, pick her up and run with her when he had always set great store on self-restraint? He only knew he was alertly on guard. There was no emotion at all on Britt's face now, yet he knew there was some deep-running emotion there. If there was to be any dissension between the two women he would most certainly be caught in the crossfire.

'I intend to, Mr. Frazer,' Natalie was saying in her politest voice. 'I'm eager and anxious to see my father and I'll try my very best not to upset him.' Those shocking blue eyes were hard on her and she decided she didn't like him at all. His glance had the brilliance of sapphires and showed very plainly how he regarded her, but it was with relief that she followed his advice. Britt appeared perfectly willing to be left alone with her cousin. It must give her great satisfaction to know she had such an ardent supporter. Lang Frazer seemed to have a great knack for extracting all kinds of confidences, though there couldn't be much left that was fresh for Britt to tell him about her errant stepdaughter.

Natalie's feet suddenly took on the wings of youth and she ran up the graceful cedar staircase, veering to the right at the landing where it divided, continuing up the short flight to her father's suite of rooms. Family portraits smiled or gazed with haughty approval down on her, but she never noticed them. She had grown up with them and now at this moment it seemed to her she had never been away, no long estrangement. Maccalla could never be a mystery to her. It knew and welcomed her, one of the few joys afforded to her for all Britt's personal ambitions. She flew along the gallery, a slender graceful creature with the light dancing over her, acting out of no sense of duty, her heart beating with no more wonderful desire than to hear the sound of her father's voice. A lack of generosity never had nor would be one of Natalie's sins, and melodramatic thoughts about her stepmother would get her nowhere. She even welcomed Lang Frazer's inevitable antagonism. Let him range himself alongside Britt, with his blue eyes as cold and sparkling as some deep trough of the sea. If he had been ready to feel contempt for her he had only half way succeeded, for somehow Natalie recognised that the cool cynicism of his sardonic expression did not cut through to his heart. It was Britt who was the wild one with unfathomable deeps, an alien in the enormous tranquillity that had been Maccalla's.

At the end of the corridor, the uniformed figure of a woman stepped out of a doorway. Natalie gained only a fleeting but favourable impression, a kind and capable woman whose brown eyes met Natalie's gravely with a look that was both searching yet gentle, for it was obvious all Natalie's attentions were turning exclusively towards her father.

Their greeting was therefore silent, all communication adequately relayed by their eyes. Janet Hood quickly reached her own decision, throwing open the door behind her and stepping to one side with something very like a blessed sigh of relief. She was immensely impressed with the young creature before her when she had been most subtly and skilfully prepared for and near prejudiced against a wilful, spoilt rotten young woman with an abominable temper. That there was temper and passion there Janet could see at a glance, but there was also sensitivity and generosity galore—she would stake her professional opinion on that. The girl's beautiful grey eyes were shimmering with tears while she cast half fearful glances through the door, one word forming yearningly in her mouth. Nothing had changed in her father's room, save the man, and Janet found her own eyes prickling.

Golden splinters of light spread around the seated figure of her patient, his long legs rooted to the ground. The breeze wafted in from the windows behind him, open to the sun and the fragrance of the garden, lightly stroking the fine, over-prominent bones of his head and his quietly folded hands.

'Natalie!'

For Andrew Calvert it was a moment of extreme self-reproach when he accepted the full measure of blame for his and his daughter's long estrangement. He had been the adult. She had been little more than a child. Now it seemed to him an agony of love was imprinted on her face and her beauty and compassion, her young frightened eagerness, her shimmering grey eyes the exact colour of his own and the thick swing of black hair, struck him like a red-hot knife.

'Natalie, my darling, forgive me!' With the words his own profound wretchedness was instantly dissipated, but the pain in his voice was apparent.

Natalie winced for him and the knowledge so cruelly brought home to her that her father's lean strong body was no longer the resilient creature it once had been, ready always to obey his commands. There was no need to wonder either whether she would break down or not. The prodigal had arrived and tears reared up in her throat, making her single: 'Papa!' sound splintered and choked. Words might have been impossible, but action was easy. She ducked her head like a charging, unseeing child, and flew across the huge room with its beautiful furnishings and its velvety soft carpet into her father's waiting embrace. His strong, good arm closed over her with a tremble and she burst into a torrent of tears.

It was that simple. She would never have let Britt drive them apart. She should have been capable of any sacrifice for love of her father, but she had acted as she did out of a fierce sense of betrayal and rejection. Now it seemed to her that her behaviour had been incredibly juvenile. They had both of them been manipulated by Britt, but no power on earth would ever make Natalie leave her father again. So she wept and wept irresistibly as anyone would who had spent five long enforced years in the wilderness, the lonely desert of no love when man's nature demanded it and the absence of it led to serious side effects.

Janet Hood stood quietly, seemingly apart yet locked in a taut triangle. She had trained herself of necessity not to become emotionally involved with her patients and their families, but she was deeply affected now. Andrew Calvert, mindful of her silent presence, lifted his dark head and smiled at her. Janet's kindness and strength rayed out to him so that he could see it and feel it as he had done from the first when Lang had brought her to him. Though what he had been through had left a mark on him it seemed to the closely observing Janet that her patient had been relieved of an intolerable burden, the burden of parental guilt he had taken on his shoulders.

'How could I, Janet?' he asked her. 'How could I have been so harshly blind to my only child? The mistakes, the *mistakes* we make! But there must be an end to them. If I had to die now with my daughter returned to me I would die willingly, with no regrets.'

Janet stared at him and a flicker of premonition struck her like a whip. 'Hush, now, hush!' she said with a quick little uprush of emotion and a warding off gesture of her hand. 'Our prayers have been answered. Now you're going to get well again.'

'Am I, Janet?' He met her eyes gravely, but there was a little smile in them and a gasp escaped Janet's mouth.

'You are. You *are!*' she said over-emphatically, and driven by a need for action she crossed the room and gently grasped Natalie's shoulders. 'Natalie, Natalie, my dear!' A tolerant and acutely intelligent woman, Janet was being caught up despite

56

herself in the tensions and intrigues of the house. She had a deep liking for her patient and a feeling of anxiety for him, and now this young creature, seemingly so fragile, with a strong look of her father, had aroused what Janet termed to herself as her 'mother hen' instincts.

With a keen professional mind and a kind heart one should be able to look forward to her patient's steady progress, instead of which Janet felt as though she was poised on the brink of a precipice, the odd time when she was overcome by her Celtic insight. Mrs. Calvert Janet heartily despised, the canny Scot in her recognising the root cause of all Mrs. Calvert's evasions and her reluctance to be with her husband. A merciful woman as she was herself, it was a form of cruelty that Janet abhorred. There were dark places in Mrs. Britt Calvert's soul, Janet sensed, some peculiar vice that was well hidden, for she was anxious and eager enough to hear reports of her husband's progress, but Janet had cut through to the heart of the matter. It was no simple case of dread of sickness and the sickroom; she had encountered enough of that in her nursing career. It was more the law of the jungle: only the fit deserved to survive. Mrs. Calvert was an exotic and unsettling creature and there was no question of any rapport between her and her husband's nurse, much less with this young stepdaughter with eyes as soft and grey as a dove's feathers. Mrs. Calvert had a flame at the centre of her long golden eyes like a burning brand. A myriad anxieties were fluttering like wings inside Janet's ribcage and she drew the girl gently to her feet, talking soothingly all the while.

'I hope I may call you that, Natalie? Welcome home, my dear. You are just what your father is needing. In fact, it's difficult to tell which one of you looks the more radiant.'

'*I* do,' said Drew Calvert, emphatically humorous, and he caught his daughter's hand, holding it fast. Natalie blinked away a few tears with the long sweep of her lashes.

'And I'll never leave you again, Papa!' she said passionately. It was obvious she was deeply affected by her homecoming and the state of her father's health, but her grey eyes as she looked up at Janet were wide and shining. 'Please do call me Natalie,' she said simply, 'and thank you for looking after my father so well. I know he's in good hands. Not just competent hands, but good, kind, dedicated hands. All the difference in the world.'

Janet experienced a sensation of quick pleasure, for the compliment was paid with such an air of sincere charm that she was irresistibly reminded of the flowerlike candour of a child. The girl was really like a lily with her exquisite matt white complexion, but Janet feared for her—which was ridiculous. She must be losing her grip, nor should she feel this heat of anxiety. She had nursed other patients through to recovery with a worse case history than Drew Calvert. From the corner of her eyes Janet saw movement. There was a quick swish and a rustle of long skirts and somehow Mrs. Calvert was among them, tall and imperious, gathering the long amber folds of her skirt, the very picture of throbbing watchfulness, her strange eyes blazing over the inexpressibly loving scene. It engulfed all of them, a living reality. Natalie's eyes like stars, trying to calm all the bittersweet sensations that were flooding her being. Britt she had always distrusted. Britt was tricky. She was dangerous and she was never troubled by scruples. She could never forget that, even if she had to banish the thought to a tiny corner of her mind. A hectic colour was over Britt's high cheekbones and even her voice, bright and welcoming, was edged with strain.

'You've had your moment, dear ones, now you must admit me into the magic circle. Lang too. Lang, *do* come up!' Sinuously Britt withdrew a few feet to the doorway, calling gaily over her shoulder, a false note somewhere in the otherwise bright cascade of sound. 'One has to practically force Lang to break up this tender scene, and it was he who brought Natalie here.' She ran her fingers through her tawny hair and the others almost heard the crackle of electricity.

You hypocrite! Janet thought, and was immediately shocked by her own reaction. Mrs. Calvert had really done nothing to justify this complete lack of charity, yet she had broken into the picture like some burningly brash intruder, leaving tension spitting and hissing like a brush fire around her. To escape her own disquietening thoughts Janet turned swiftly to watch Lang Frazer's entry into the room. He was Mrs. Calvert's cousin, but he had proved himself a very good friend to her patient, and the warm smile in Drew Calvert's eyes as he took the

59

hand of the younger man settled the matter for Janet.

'Good to see you back, Lang. I can't thank you enough. For everything!'

'I don't want to intrude, Drew, now that I've seen Natalie home again.'

'As though you could! Janet, with your approval I propose to break open a bottle of champagne. My heart is full enough, so it won't matter if I forgo my share.'

'That will be grand!' Britt seconded in a voice so bright it went oddly with the icy stiffening of her body. 'Apparently Natalie is just the tonic we've all been needing. I'm awfully sorry, Miss Hood, but I'll have to ask you to fetch the champagne for us. Cook's night off, you know, and no way of persuading her to change her plans,' she explained with an apologetic smile that had not a trace of friendliness in it.

I've made an enemy there! Janet thought dismally, and why now, this minute, particularly? Was it so apparent that she had already gone over to the other side? The return of the prodigal daughter represented adverse conditions to Mrs. Calvert. Janet glanced at her patient in the unconsciously easy fashion of one who had reached a complete liking and understanding of the other, a quiet, serious friendliness and mutual respect. 'One glass wouldn't hurt you, I should think!'

'That would be lovely, though I'm intoxicated enough having Natalie home again.'

Across the intervening space Natalie met a pair of blue eyes into which brilliant shining depths she could fall. An infinity of sensation was sparking off within her, so disturbing she closed her eyes; she couldn't help it, strangely reluctant to hold that iridescent, unreachable glance. His presence must inevitably excite and disturb her like a sparkling clear flow to the brain. She must conclude now, right at the beginning, that they could never be friends—if indeed friendship was possible with such an essentially sensuous man, the expression on his dark face hardening with controlled cynicism every time he looked at her. There was only one way they could ever communicate, and the brilliant fearful thought made her betray herself so that she clutched at her father's chair for support, speaking a little shakily with considerable effort, conscious of Britt's brittle gaze like a glass barrier between them. 'Let me get it, *please*! And why not dinner? I'm a very good cook and unabashed to admit it, and Papa could. . . .' She broke off, hesitating, with the most sensitive awareness that her father was rallying—but perhaps too much stimulation would be unwise.

'It's all right, darling,' her father said gently. 'My health is quite equal to what my heart is feeling. I've rested enough this afternoon,' he continued with some spirit, because it was quite untrue, 'and now I'm wide awake and looking forward to enjoying a good dinner downstairs. Why not set it up in the morning room, then we can be closer together and enjoy the lights of the city below. You will stay, Lang? You make life so much easier and you can't let me down. Besides, I've an idea Natalie is going to do us proud.'

'That should make us all content with our lot,' Lang Frazer said with a lazy smile. 'To look superlative—and now this!' He gave Natalie his total attention, his smile accentuating the curve of his mouth. He had adopted an attitude of witty, amused indulgence towards her that Natalie knew was for her father's benefit alone. 'As a matter of fact, Natalie, I'll come along with you and see what the kitchen has to offer. I'm fairly knowledgeable myself. Shall we say dinner at eight, then that won't rush either of us. The sauce might prove tricky.'

Andrew Calvert gave a short bark of amusement. 'Just as long as it doesn't bother Natalie. Two cooks in the kitchen, Lang! You're much too big to pitch headlong out.'

'For heaven's sake, Drew, with your daughter surely I'm quite safe. It would be extremely awkward of Natalie to try it in any case, she's a featherweight! Now if you're all reassured, we professionals will take ourselves off. You can get that splendid robe of yours out, Drew. I've always admired it and the occasion calls for it. I'll use the Boue guest room again, if I may. I've taken quite a fancy to the opaline collection. It goes with my eyes,' he tacked on flippantly, three of him reflected in the triple full-length Sheraton mirror.

'No, it doesn't!' Natalie broke out, staring. 'The colour maybe, but not the opaque glazing. Your eyes are brilliant—breathtaking, very sheer and sparkling.'

He spun on her abruptly, breaking up his reflections. '*Glassy*, are you trying to say, Natalie?'

They were playing a game and she knew it, presenting a smooth front that gave Britt, at least, no satisfaction. 'I can see no reason why you should have to mess about in the kitchen, Lang. If the worst comes to the worst I can help Natalie out myself, though I can't pretend I'm much of a hand.'

'Well, that settles it!' Lang Frazer said blandly. 'I'm rather particular about what I eat. Let us do it for you, Britt. It's reward enough, I know, to have Drew with us downstairs.'

'Well, that's taken care of, then,' said Britt, recovering, her long narrow eyes ranging over Natalie and her cousin. 'I'll rest myself—there's been precious little of it for me. You don't need me, dearest?'

'Thank you, no.' Drew Calvert smiled at his wife with absolutely no expression in his eyes. 'Janet will look after me and get my robe out. Noël Coward wouldn't have scorned it, if I say so myself!'

'With all due respect, Noël Coward wasn't handsome like you, Papa. You're the best looking man I've seen!'

'You should get a slap for that!' Lang Frazer suddenly pinned Natalie's slender wrist, thoroughly disconcerting her. 'I know you're only saying it for Drew's benefit. Now the things my various women friends have told me. . . .' He drew her fingers locked about her to the door. 'See you all later, then. Drew, Britt, Janet, you're with us, of course?'

'Wild horses couldn't keep me from this one!'

'Precisely!' He lifted one black eyebrow at Janet and withdrew, once out of the room shifting his firm, easy grip to Natalie's arm. 'Please don't quiver like a runaway filly!'

63

'Am I acting like that?' she challenged him. 'I could have sworn you take no account of my reactions at all.'

'Natalie!' he taunted dryly, and something in his jewelled glance made her colour.

'You don't have to help me,' she protested. 'For all I know you may hopelessly outclass me.'

'At most things undoubtedly, but not cooking, my girl. Don't delude yourself you're going to have a helpmate there.'

She stopped in astonishment, staring up at him. 'But you said ... oh well, that's glad tidings anyway. I don't think I could stand your piercing scrutiny overseeing things.'

'You'll stand it all right, and shame on you. The very idea of a beautiful girl being able to turn out a decent meal absolutely fascinates me. I'll just check around to see it doesn't come out of tins. Though why the devil Vera should choose to take the evening off I'll never know. To the best of my knowledge she hasn't had an evening off in three years.'

'Perhaps she has a lot of old gossip, recipes, anything to catch up on. If I tell you your fears are groundless and my cooking won't turn you to stone, will you stay here? I can't see why you offered at all in the first place unless you're given to making idle boasts.'

'Never idle, Natalie, calculated. I just had the idea I had to catch you up from the scene of an accident. You have that effect on me, but why I can't say. I don't normally feel that way, though heaven knows you vastly appeal to my eye. Perhaps that's it.'

'Then why the big wedge between us—and there is one?'

'Don't start that again,' he warned her. 'The main problem has been solved. Drew looks better than we ever dared hope. There's been some curious frailty of the spirit about him that's driven us all frantic. Be good to him, Natalie of the raven hair, or God help you!'

'It's as well you're very zealous on account of my father, otherwise I mightn't take all the punishment you're determined to hand out to me,' she said sweetly.

'Why, does it hurt you so much, you silly little goose? Why, if you hadn't claimed to have lifted your cooking to an art form I wouldn't bother with you at all.'

She stared up at him uncertainly, his dark face so handsome and mocking, rather ruthlessly intent on her, she tried to jolt her arm from his grip.

'Forget it, Natalie! An excellent suggestion. I'm coming along with you. This has always been a house of plenty—excessive indulgence in some ways. I rarely eat more than once a day, it's all I seem to get time for, but I do like black coffee. Unless you're better than both of us think, don't try to outdo Vera. She's a very virtuous, unsentimental spinster but a veritable Circe in the kitchen. Her dinner parties are sumptuous!'

'For which Britt gets all the credit.'

'Doesn't the hostess always get the credit, little cat?'

'Give me a little time and I'll dazzle you yet,' Natalie assured him.

'You're dazzling me *now*, would you only know it! My thirst for beauty is generally acknowledged to be extravagant, and you're a lovely thing, Natalie of the gauzy eyes.'

'But you don't believe in *me*?' They were passing through the hallway that led out to the kitchen and she came to a halt, staring up at him as though without his answer she refused to go a step further.

'No, not as yet, little one!' he said, considering her, some flame in his blue eyes that completely dispelled the illusion of friendship he had been creating for her. 'You have to prove yourself in all sorts of ways. But it's true I am feeling a little kindlier disposed towards you this evening.'

'I've only faintly noticed it!' she said, trying to walk on.

'Have you? Well, that's one frail bond between us. On you, young Natalie, we all depend. You can make or break your father, bring him back to health or destroy him.'

'How could you!' She swung about a little recklessly and Lang caught the point of her shoulder to steady her. 'You're determined to question me, aren't you? My motives. Can't you see how much I love my father, how sick and shaken I am to see him so physically reduced?'

'I *do* see it,' he answered, meeting her gaze very directly and pushing the thick shining hair off her shoulder. 'But love pulls us in many ways, Natalie. It's a powerful force that can just as easily be misdirected as work for us and the ones we love. You're not free from prejudice. *You* know it and *I* know it, and it could make for storms ahead.'

'And you're something else again! You hate me!' Her silvery eyes were full on his face, wide and shaken.

'I don't!' he said, gently sardonic, 'but Britt is my cousin and Drew is my friend. None of us are as important to him as you are, and don't catch your breath. Things aren't quite right between Britt and your father, I know that, but any conflict between you and Britt must inevitably involve me, and what I'm most concerned about, pull down your father.'

'I'll do everything I can to avert it,' said Natalie, feeling truly faint.

'Well, why speak as though it's all foreordained?'

'Don't you believe in destiny?' she asked softly, moving away from him, opening the door to the streamlined, gleaming kitchen and making a little wry face. It had lost all its old character in what appeared to be extensive remodelling. Lang Frazer had followed her, his blue eyes so fantastically alive that the impulse to resist him flamed up in her.

'Go away!' she said like a wild thing, lifting back the heavy dark sweep of her hair.

'*No*, though for some reason you're trying to make me lose my detachment.'

'But you're not detached, are you, you said so yourself.' Her eyes travelled with faint interest over the double ovens, refrigerator, freezer wall and on to the centre cooking island. Excitement was licking along her veins like fire and she wished she was alone to calm herself. 'Do you know,' she said, and her words came out like a soft sigh she scarcely

67

wished on herself, 'I have a long dress the exact colour of your eyes. I'll wear it for dinner.'

'That might boomerang on yourself,' said Lang, and his hand closed on her nape to turn her round to him. 'I'm a lot older than you, Natalie, and that alone should tell you something.'

'I thought our relations were strained enough without worrying about anything else,' she said in a rush, possessed of a strange urgency that was making her lean towards him instead of evading him.

He tipped up her chin, an odd light in the depths of his eyes, his face hard, full of vitality and power. 'No resistance, Natalie?'

'Would it do me any good?'

'No.' His hands closed over her shoulders and he drew her to him. 'On one thing we can agree, this was bound to happen, so let's get it over. Your expression relates almost exactly to your thoughts. Physical attraction can easily enslave all of us, but I'm very effectively armoured.'

'Then why kiss me?' she queried, her head tilted back like a flower.

'A momentary compulsion. Close your eyes, then you'll be free of me. I promise I had no such thought in my head until you started provoking me.'

'I don't believe you!'

'I don't believe myself,' he said, his eyes brilliant. 'If you're going to fight me, now's the time.'

Some elemental antagonism seemed to prowl in him, turning his eyes to blue fire so that she tilted her small chin and spoke very softly and urgently. 'It must be a bizarre sensation, wanting to kiss a woman you don't trust!'

'Did I say I wanted to, Natalie?'

'I'm sorry,' she gave a funny little shake of her head, 'I thought you did!' The light shone directly into her shimmering, liquid eyes, illuminating her flowerlike skin. Excitement and the faint sense of strain he engendered in her only served to heighten her extreme femininity, so that he gave a muffled exclamation that might have been 'damnation' and threaded his hand into her hair, twisting a heavy silken skein, forcing her head into the curve of his shoulder.

His mouth as it found hers unerringly was as strangely punitive as it was ravishing, as though he saw himself the unwilling victim of her allurement, that mysterious force that was urging him to lock her still closer until she was shaking in his arms with a frightening desire that had sprung up from nowhere, unable to move, yielding and ardent, when she should have been running away.

When he released her she said his name in a soft, dreamlike trance, as though she had only to turn her head for the excitement to begin again, a fine blaze of emotion that was making her heart beat in great agitation. 'God knows where you learned to kiss like that,' he said, instantly alienating her.

Her mouth was throbbing, warm and alive, the taunt in his voice making her delicate nostrils flare. 'For some reason it's important to you to torment me!'

'Oh, God, what nonsense!' he said a little angrily. 'You're beautiful and you inspire hunger in a man. Now unless we're going to be miserably unhappy together let's separate before I kiss you again—and don't say you don't ask for it. Perhaps we've both learnt a lesson, without wanting it, we're each able to arouse the other. I for one am prepared to sacrifice my own inclinations for the good of my soul. You really get to a man, and that in itself can do a lot of harm.'

'You brute of a bachelor!' she snapped, stung by his splendid male arrogance, all the more distressing in such an extraordinarily attractive man. She was filled with a wonderful sense that she could quite comfortably shun him unless he touched her again. Incredible to think she had known such incomparable excitement in his arms. But she could resist him, every single distraction he offered, the vivid flowering blue wilderness of his eyes, the curve of his mouth, the intensely elegant set of his body.

'I suppose I knew, Natalie, the first moment I saw you, that you'd be a major disruptive element in my life.'

'If that's the case I'm quite content!' she said stormily. 'It would be glorious to give you a few headaches. Now get out of my kitchen, you're dangerous.'

Whatever Lang's failings a lack of humour wasn't one of them. He smiled and it was extraordinarily attractive, the hard, unyielding expression wiped clear of his face. 'I suppose it was too much to hope we could join forces. All right, Natalie, now I've put you on the right track, I'll go! We're all becoming a little over-emotional, and that's not to be wondered at, though the two of us anywhere could lead to complications, I expect.'

'If that's true, it's your fault!' she burst out defiantly, 'though I have to admit you're a very stylish tormentor.'

'If you say so,' he countered suavely, his expression sardonic again. 'Be of good cheer, Natalie, my changeling, I'm going. After all, a dinner party for five isn't that many. Naturally if anyone enquires I expect you to give me half the credit.'

'We'll all enjoy it the more for thinking it!' she said sweetly, then looked very serious all of a sudden. 'You *do* think Father is up to it?'

'Be convinced, child!' he said gently. 'It's what he very much wants and it represents progress.' He paused for a moment, looking down at her very searchingly, her head tilted on its slender curving neck. 'The one thing we don't want is trouble, so Natalie, *behave!*'

'I will if you will!' She returned his gaze rather broodingly, resolutely avoiding the curve of his mouth.

Abruptly he reached out and trailed a silky strand of hair around her throat. 'Some women are born to make trouble—a hard lesson I guess every man has found out. Now if you're going to make preparations for dinner, I suggest you get on with it. I shall try to ignore any of your mistakes.'

'How gracious!' she said lightly, but he was already gone. Hours later, after dinner, as they all lingered idly over their coffee, Natalie saw the light of amused congratulations in Lang's eyes. If a challenge had been presented, she had certainly risen to it, which all came from having a French grandmother who took cooking very seriously. The soft lighting caught her in a pool of light and blue eyes lingered rather mockingly on her beautiful hyacinthine dress in a silky sheer chiffon with a diminutive low curving top. Against the deep blue her skin gleamed with the lustre of a pearl and a silver flower on a fine chain swung between the tender curves of her breasts.

The last trace of strain had left her father's dear face and on a quick heartfelt impulse she reached across and took his hand to lift it to her face. 'It's wonderful to be home again, Papa!'

'Amen, my darling.'

From the top of the table with its lovely lace place mats, its lustrous heirloom silver and fine china, the low centrepiece of tiny white flowers, Britt Calvert leaned back and blew cigarette smoke heavily through her nose. The blood glittered in her veins, charging her face with her own curious unreciprocated feelings and the effects of the wine. She had lived so long with the false hope that this girl would never come back and her golden eyes glowed vehemently bright. All her senses were gathered to the point where she felt like screaming out her bitter enmity towards this girl who could make so many difficulties in her life.

Damn you, *damn you*, how dare you come back! The glowing amber eyes filled with thwarted tears that she remembered as the attentions of the table turned to her to declare as a sincere, loving desire to make a new beginning. Janet alone sensed the ambivalence in her, and now after a delicious meal and the satisfaction of seeing her patient looking so relaxed and happy it was almost as stunning as having a dagger thrown at one. With such concealed violence in the house if she had any sense at all she would jet off somewhere else, but she could scarcely leave her patient. Neither, she now found, could she desert the daughter with her young face full of pure joy, holding her father's hand, her light eyes shimmering like stars.

People could and did die of broken hearts, Janet had found, and before his daughter had been returned to him, Andrew Calvert had lost his attachment to life. Now instead of remorse he had his daughter to put in its place. Janet made a silent vow that it would stay that way, at the very least until her patient was well again.

CHAPTER THREE

In the weeks ahead Andrew Calvert established and maintained such a steady rate of progress that shortly before Christmas he was able to get about for quite lengthy periods with the aid of a stick. The mornings were the worst, he wryly informed them, when his limbs, especially his legs, felt as though they had been filled with lead, incapable of independent action without his exerting short, terrific bursts of will power, mind over the frailty of the body, the burning up of nervous energy that eventually tired him out. He went to bed early, but he was up for most of the day. As he was a member of the sophisticated élite and one of the city's most distinguished architects his recovery was greeted with sincere pleasure and relief as though a niggling burden that had been placed on all of his friends' shoulders had suddenly been lifted. An urbane, very courteous man of exceptional gifts, Andrew Calvert had genuinely endeared himself to his fellows, something quite outside the reach of most of us.

Even Britt's wretchedness and neurotic planning was temporarily abated as with Natalie in the house she could once more, with a clear conscience, pick up the social threads of her life. Mrs. Britt Calvert had endured purgatory long enough and her absence had wonderful compensations. With Britt out of the house, often and for long periods, including the occasional overnight stay in their city unit, Natalie and her father were blissfully happy. Janet, who kept a sharp inexplicably anxious eye on her patient but tactfully kept out of the way a good deal, felt they both thoroughly deserved it. She had no idea of the cause of the five-year estrangement, but it took no great informed guess to realise that Mrs. Calvert had more than a little to do with it. Andrew Calvert's joy in the return of his daughter was so clearly expressed in his returning health and the message in his fine eyes, the barrier that had once been there, was no more, neither of them referring to it again. It was a wonderful argument for the senselessness of all family arguments. Blood always was and always would be thicker than water, for which many a parent and child would be forever grateful.

With his return to wellbeing, Andrew Calvert felt a resurgence of interest in his work again. Lang had borne the brunt of it long enough, he exclaimed, though heaven knows Lang had the enormous strength and the extraordinary amount of energy necessary to see all the Calvert, Frazer, Duncan projects were brought to completion. Lang Frazer, Natalie's father was fond of telling her, was a true architect, combining a great sense of imagination with a mastery of all the latest technology. Both of them, even if he said it himself, were highly accomplished, including 'Young Duncan', whom Natalie had to meet, but Lang had a single, individual style that was immediately recognizable. Lang Frazer had a great future and Andrew Calvert liked to think he had given him a start at a time when other senior architects felt, quite rightly perhaps, that the younger man would soon overshadow them. A man of stature himself, Andrew Calvert had never feared this, and before his illness the work had been pouring in for all of them. It was recognised, however, that only Lang had the fantastic energy to carry the firm and supervise the completion of Andrew Calvert's own buildings and private houses.

In this way Lang was in and out of Maccalla almost every other day but never at a set time, only when he found the spare moment to confer with his partner. Strangely, his visits seemed to coincide with the times his cousin was out of the house and Natalie, if no one else, was very thankful. Britt's manner towards her had proved consistently cool and composed, but Natalie felt a throbbing uneasiness in her stepmother's presence—a kind of defence mechanism, she supposed, for she had been badly hurt before and the pain had been stamped on her brain like a permanent warning.

During Lang's visits Natalie herself kept out of the way. Time was a precious commodity to him and none of them wanted to tire her father unduly. Besides, she viewed Lang Frazer with some trepidation. There was no peace with *him*! He was too clever and so diabolically sure of himself that even her father smiled in appreciative enjoyment and the half-formed wish to tell the younger man to slow down, there was no real race to win even if Lang was a thoroughbred and half the pleasure in life was winning. His emphasis and energy, the dark sparkling vitality, were so much in evidence these days it made them all feel a little aimless.

It was with a sense of shock then that Natalie found him actually seeking her out. So totally transfixed was she, so totally surprised by his challenging and unexpected presence in the library where she was placing a bronze container of perfect yellow roses, her hand flung up against a thorny stem. The tiny spurt of pain was the only reason she so quickly found her voice.

'Oh!' Childishly she put the smarting wound to her mouth.

'I'm sorry, Natalie!' he murmured sardonically, his brilliant blue eyes leaping over her. 'Did *I* do that to you?' He covered the extra pace towards her and caught her wrist, holding up her hand for his inspection. 'Just a prick!'

'Well, it hurt, but I didn't really expect any sympathy.' Warm colour was tingeing her cheekbones and her heart began its now familiar racing. Why did he make her feel as if she had to marshal all her resistance against him, especially now when he was smiling, a disturbing, frankly mocking light in his vivid eyes. She snatched her hand away abruptly as if his touch seared her, which in its way it did. 'All your business completed?' she enquired, striving for the light touch and finding it extraordinarily difficult.

'Hmmm!' His deep drawl called attention to the attractive, very resonant timbre of his voice.

'Father's doing wonderfully well, isn't he?'

'For which we all have to thank you,' he agreed with a smile, and a real smile this time, none of his cat-and-mouse stuff. His hand came down on the table with an air of finality. 'Finish that arrangement, Natalie, you're dithering anyway. If you move another rose a fraction of an inch to the right or the left the whole thing will collapse.'

She shook her head darkly. 'I never know quite what to do when you're around.'

'And I like it that way!' he said instantly, as if he was running out of patience when he didn't have a lot. He tipped a finger to her chin and turned her face to him. 'Manners, Natalie—I thought you were a nicely brought up little girl and I want to talk to you. Drew tells me he's going to rest for an hour or so and then Janet has some exercise programme lined up for him, so you may take the rest of the day off. With me,' he added succinctly.

'You take my breath away!' she said shakily, which was no less than the truth, and she put it down to extra years and his driving masculinity.

'Well, I've seen you like that before, breathless!' he pointed out rather unkindly, his blue eyes when they chose to be flaring into sensual life.

'Am I to understand you're taking me somewhere?' she said a little woodenly, regretting the fact that he could almost reduce her to gibberish.

'Yes!' Laconically he lifted his hand and patted her cheek as if she was a parrot he had successfully taught a lesson. 'I'm taking you out to Bellwood, one of our new housing projects—nothing terribly original or ambitious. Designing original houses is pretty unprofitable in lots of ways. I've found I have to reserve my original ideas for very private people with a certain life style. It can be a very personal experience and expensive. However, this particular project is pretty good of its kind. I want you to see it and so does your father. I must say I'm interested and fascinated to learn you've played down your own talents. Your father doesn't seem to know a great deal about your professional capabilities, which I'd tell you are not inconsiderable if I didn't think it would turn your head.'

Natalie flashed him an unconcerned glance, then answered quite truthfully. 'I don't think my father has been well enough so far to discuss them properly. It's almost as if he's come back from a long way, a withdrawal from life. I think my just being here has been enough for him up to date.'

'Yes,' he agreed with a smile, and a glance of approval, 'I have to concede that you grace the house in more ways than one. There's only one little change I'd like to make—that sundress, or whatever it's supposed to be. My imagination gets quite enough outlet and the workmen on the site are finding their jobs rewarding enough. I couldn't tell you what some of them take out in their pay packets. Now when you're ready to go—nothing prettier, of course, just something less beguiling. An hour or so out at the site, then lunch on the way back. I have just the place lined up and you've been a fairly good girl....'

'.... which even *you* have to accept,' she interrupted him.

'What do you mean, *even* I, Natalie?' His quick eyes narrowed over her. 'I'm not your adversary.'

'Oh? I'd got used to thinking you were.'

'Have no fear, I'll love you yet!'

'*Words*, Mr. Frazer, what man could be without

them! Besides, I appreciate the fact that you're a bachelor at heart!'

'You're mad!' he protested, half amused, half irritated. 'I'm only waiting for the right woman.'

'Who hasn't turned up yet?'

'Forgive me if I don't answer that one, but I will tell you my phone runs hot. I'm currently in high favour on the matrimonial lists.'

'Which just goes to show women have a taste for trouble.'

'I've learned that, my child!' he said, and his eyes were quite brilliant with mockery. 'But tell me, are you coming or not? I seldom reissue invitations—and think of the waiting list!'

'Why not?' she smiled at him, and her own eyes were dancing. 'I can guarantee you *I* won't interfere with your freedom.'

'My darling girl, I don't put you in the category of my women friends. Be out at the car in under ten minutes.'

'I can be ready in eight.'

'I'm counting from now,' he said, moving briskly away from her with his sleek, co-ordinated movements, catching up a briefcase neatly from the gilt console table in the hallway. For a moment Natalie stared after him, utterly distracted, then she cleared her whirling head with a quick little shake and hurried out of the library, up the divided stairway and out to her room in the west wing. She felt burningly alive, flooded with pleasure and anticipation. Houses were her own world, after all, and she felt she had something worthwhile to contribute. If the truth were known, with no one other than her father would she care to look over such a project than Lang Frazer. A devilish, autocratic, sarcastic, keep-you-right-on-your-toes sort of man he might be, but she realised quite an honour had been accorded her. It would be difficult indeed not to be flattered. Already he had received considerable recognition as a brilliant creative architect who could fully exploit form and all and essential ingredients that went to make up a noteworthy architect. Only that day her father had told her that Lang had a king-size talent and with it the ability to influence others, so she would have to respond with the proper, respectful demeanour.

When she reached the Mercedes his eyes approved her chic little skirt and top with gorgeous peony flowers on the skirt and a plain silky top in a blue fragment of the wonderful colours of the skirt. Her high sandals were the same beautiful bluebell. She slid into the expensive pigskin upholstery and he glanced at her legs, then her feet, appreciatively.

'Very nice, Natalie. The first thing I noticed about you—your lovely limbs.'

'Thank you.'

'Tell me, did you always have this penchant for blue?'

'To be honest, only since I met you. Now I wonder why I bother with any other colour. It's so heavenly.'

He laughed and regarded her steadily, and the quality of his glance made her smooth back the heavy forward sweep of her hair and make herself small in her seat. 'I shouldn't do this, provoke you!'

'That's right, Natalie. Not too heavy on the flower power.'

'I'm all attention now,' she assured him, folding her narrow hands. 'A career woman mindful of the great honour being done her.'

Lang appeared to consider the 'career woman' gravely, then he laughed, a low, faintly derisive sound. 'That's a tall order for you, isn't it, little one? A career woman?'

'Why on earth should it be?' she demanded.

'Why on earth do you swing your hair like that, or wear your clothes with such flair, or use your eyes so outrageously?'

'Do you mean to say it isn't consistent with successfully pursuing a career? Can't you see me a career woman?'

'I can't see who'd let you!' he qualified with a long level stare, as he reversed expertly out of the drive. 'What about Adrian now? Wasn't that your boss's name, Adrian?'

'Yes,' she said, sounding a little resentful, and not adding anything to it.

'A thought-provoking silence. Is Adrian married already, or has he asked you to marry him?'

'We've discussed it,' she said shortly.

'Only recently?'

'Yes.'

'You're a mine of information. Let's widen the list more. How many others?'

'None that matter,' she said. 'I've no intention of getting married for years yet.'

Lang glanced at her briefly and she turned away with fresh urgency. 'It must be coming increasingly obvious to you, Natalie, unless you can keep running that's going to be an extremely difficult thing to do—and you may quote me if you like. You're much too lovely and you have style and intelligence. Marrying you off will be no problem at all.'

'I'd rather make a success of my career,' she insisted. 'It shouldn't bother the high seats of power. Interior design is a relatively feminine area. I've no talent for nursing like Janet, though I suppose I could have been a schoolteacher or a librarian or whatever else that's allowed.'

'The thing is,' he asked steadily, 'is that what you really want, a career, or are you just pleasurably filling in time? I can't accept that a truly female woman can sustain the high degree of commitment necessary to hold down an exacting and expert position. You know yourself your own boss was a man and I'm sure he was very good at his job. There are very few women at the top and plenty of reasons for it. Just being a woman must rule out being totally involved with a career. Most women want children. They insist on getting married even these days. If they do go out and get a job it's only to provide their families with a few luxuries or they have to do it to make ends meet or they're going quietly mad at home and prefer making the teas and typing up a few letters, but there's only a small part of them actually committed to the job. That's why a lot of women settle down happily to routine, so they can rattle on happily about their love lives or what sort of a rough time their husband is giving them.'

'I take it you don't believe in career women, then?'

'No, Natalie, I don't. Nothing personal, I assure you—just a few friends who've struck trouble with dual careers. They're all divorced now and no happier, when it would have been simplicity itself to jettison one career and save the marriage. It's hard, I know, for the woman always being the noble one, but there must be the rewards, surely? Fill in your time creatively and settle for marriage. It will be much easier, and if you're a smart girl, which you are, there should be all the fulfilment in the world. You don't really need me to fill you in on the illuminating facts. Thousands of women would sacrifice their careers to get married next spring.'

'Well, why shouldn't you want to get married as well?'

'My darling girl!' He looked across at her, pained. 'I told you—I'm already married to my job. The woman who would be prepared to take me on would be exceptional.'

'Agreed.'

'And no need to be impertinent.'

'I never was!' she protested, turning lake-coloured eyes on him. 'I only meant what woman could measure up?'

'Don't you think before you open that soft, sweet mouth?' he asked dryly.

'If I did, we would have no conversation at all. With you I react, not answer—something quite primitive, for all I consider myself civilised and I'm sure you do too!'

'My dear girl!' Lang said feelingly, 'men and

women are never really civilised in their dealings with one another. We've learned absolutely nothing since we came out of the caves. I, for instance, would just like to pick you up and head into the daisies. Fortunately I'm a career man and I have an appointment with our builder in about twenty-five minutes.'

'Now that's what I call a high degree of commitment,' she said admiringly, and earned a searing blue glance for herself.

'You'll be looking for cover, Natalie, before the day's out!'

'Then I'll take good care not to waste one precious moment!'

They were making the descent from the foothills and Natalie turned her head to look out at the scenery because she loved it and it worked its own magic. It meant something inexpressibly harmonious to her, like a painting or a piece of music or some beautiful object she prized, though it could still hurt her with old memories. Everything that had happened to her came back to Maccalla. The countryside was very quiet with the peculiar golden stillness, the drowsy warmth, of summer, and she experienced a sensation of wonderful security as though she had found the right place for her alone. They were moving swiftly past the green waves of trees, the fields and the vineyards that breathed peace and plenty, and her eyes, had she known it, had the silvery clarity of the prisms in Maccalla's great chandeliers.

'You love it here, don't you?' asked Lang, abruptly breaking the silence.

'Of course I do!'

'Maccalla perhaps has too much of an influence on you. Won't you mind when you go away again? When you marry, I mean, so stop all those delicate little jumps.'

'I don't think I could bear it if I couldn't come back from time to time,' she said quite seriously.

'You'll have your work cut out finding a husband to accommodate such a wandering fancy.'

'But I *told* you,' she said, trying to speak lightly, 'I don't want a husband. I'll find plenty of other things to fill in my time.'

'It would be absurd to make a house a major cause for disagreement. It's obvious, Natalie, you feel very passionately about your home.'

'It's extremely important to me, yes,' she agreed, looking for the first time bewildered.

'That's what I thought!' he said tersely, sounding as if he couldn't stop himself either. 'Here's hoping you find a suitable male to tolerate your fateful addiction.'

'I'm trying *my* best to maintain good relations,' she pointed out quickly, 'while you haven't been quite civilised to me since you arrived. The thing is, you're absolutely disenchanted with women.'

'I'm still under your spell, Natalie!' He smiled at her, but there was no humour in his eyes. It was a curiously tense moment and Natalie found she couldn't sustain it. She pressed her head back against the head rest, shutting her eyes and giving a faint regretful sigh. 'No, Lang Frazer, I can't mark *you* down as a romantic, and you don't like me at all!'

86

'Let's leave it, shall we? For now!'

She stole a quick glance at him, uncertain of his mood, then shut her eyes again, behind her closed lids the sun-blazoned image of him still flickering, the exact angle of his head, the firm chin, the clear cut of his mouth and the cool irony in his eyes. He was a rip-roaring cynic, an out-and-out woman-hater, and he really deserved to have his feelings reciprocated. So demoralising to know that wasn't the response he aroused in her.

Silence seemed the best solution. In just under the half hour they reached the tree-studded development, a fine tract of land that had once been a farm. Six houses stood in light, semi-secluded bushland and two more were awaiting roofing with workmen clambering all over them. Natalie looked about her with extreme interest as they cruised past the big sign that announced a Hayes-Murray project designed by Calvert, Frazer & Duncan. Her immediate impression was that the whole project was admirable, a complete breakthrough from even good suburbia and a surprisingly beautiful environment with only the initial landscaping attempted. The houses were recognisably and distinctively Australian, uniquely sun-orientated, protecting, sheltering, at the same time making stimulating architectural statements. Much use had been made of redwood and stained cedar and silvery grey shakes, but one house in particular was almost sculptural with its positive white stuccoed walls and dark-stained timber. It had a special feeling of dynamism that in the strong sunlight made it look quite splendid.

'Now that I like!' she said, turning her head. 'It's very arresting, yet it's welcoming. I want to see inside.'

'All right! We'll start there. I'll have a word with Bart Hayes first. I'd like you to meet him. The business, I feel, is moving towards a conglomerate corporation. It *must* come, and I'd like Hayes, Murray along with us. They're good and they know how to translate ideas. I'm just waiting until Drew feels a little stronger to discuss the whole idea. The old days have gone for good,' he went on. 'The unhurried, highly personalised touch. There's a tremendous amount of pressure these days like turning out projects like this, quality homes but within the reach of the middle income. Only a certain section of the population can afford significant design, though I find working to a reasonable budget a challenge. We're here to survive and we've got to be business men as least as good as the business firms for which we design. For my own part I've found it's paid off to be able to erect a house myself as distinct from designing the plans. It's taken the devil of a long time playing down the dilettante architect. Plenty of builders and developers dispense with the services of an architect, and naturally I don't go along with that. It seems kind of mindless, or aesthetically unacceptable, and one sees so much usable space either wasted or ignored. Bart Hayes used us right from the start and he heads one of our biggest construction companies. What we have to ensure is that we don't lose him or hold him up or increase costs. So far, even with Drew incapacitated we've avoided all three.'

'And you haven't approached Father?'

'So far no. He hasn't been well enough. Then too, Natalie, and I expect you to respect my confidence, your father was brought up to a certain standard of living—a gracious, very mellow existence, the gentleman architect with his equally well off client. Up until now he has resisted everything that smacks of "impersonal". The only flaw in the whole thing is that the whole profession has been revolutionized. I want to approach Drew with my ideas, gradually. Hayes, of course, is all for bulldozing in, but I know your father and I admire and respect him. I don't want him hurried, but at the same time we must change direction to exploit our ideas fully and make a maximum contribution to the architecture of the country. Builders like Hayes are going along with the architects and that's what I want, no desperate efforts by builders to throw up everything and anything.'

'Well, no one could say that of these houses,' Natalie agreed.

'I hope not,' he shrugged his powerful shoulders. 'They're eminently satisfactory designs, extremely liveable with no valuable space ignored. Different in design, of course, but they present a coherent pattern.'

'That one, perhaps, has set the standard for the rest,' Natalie said, gesturing towards the white, sculptured building.

'Maybe!' he said nonchalantly, 'but a little more individual, Natalie, and it would have been very hard to sell. Frustrating, but in general, true.'

'It's yours?'

'That one was spontaneous,' he said, nodding. 'Don't take it as truly representative of my work. It can't be. I simply can't attempt too emphatic a statement here. We're all of us working to set specifications, but it's good of its kind and it's safe. Instant appeal to the right kind of people. If you want to see one of my so-called prestige private homes I'll take you out to Magda Franks' place. It's nearing completion.'

'Magda Franks, the concert pianist?'

'Yes. She's coming back home for her retirement. It will be ready for her when she arrives. I knew Magda well in London and she's given me carte blanche, which isn't to say she doesn't know exactly what she wants. I'm just giving it to her that much better.'

'I'd certainly love to see it.'

'Well, no limit on the budget helps.' Lang came around to Natalie's side of the car and helped her out, steering her towards one of the unfinished houses.

'Magda Franks was a career woman,' she couldn't resist saying.

'Magda, my child,' he pointed out, looking down his nose at her, 'is a brilliant artist, and one must always make an exception of artists. At the same time she has two broken marriages behind her.'

'I didn't know that!' Natalie said artlessly, 'and I've read a great deal about her.'

'She doesn't advertise the fact on the sleeves of her records, but it's true enough. Besides, you're not old enough to know everything. I'm only being kind in saying so.'

'You're not kind at all.'

'No, not to you. Now, Harry Banks, the landscaper,' he said, tightly gripping her arm as if to ward off her escape, 'has been working with us right from the beginning. Down there will be parkland, and as you can see all the streets run down to it with a common ride to the rear of the houses. Where we possibly can we've done away with fences and where they're absolutely necessary they'll be planted in depth. All of the houses have enclosed antriums for complete privacy and Harry will move in next week with his plantings. He supervised the bulldozing and marked out all the native gums and pines for saving. All his introduced exotics will be super advanced. The landscaping links the whole thing. The houses are quite different, but they have a unifying feel. Drew and I have always worked well together and Bruce Duncan is a very talented youngster. It's been quite a source of satisfaction to us to know the whole project is exciting a lot of interest in the business. Soon we'll let the public in, the really important ones.

'Well, they can't fail to appreciate what you've done here. It seems a giant step forward to me.'

'With interior design,' he amended. 'We intend to do over one or two houses as showcases. All houses look better furnished. Ah, here's Bart. Smile prettily, Natalie, as befitting Drew Calvert's daughter.'

'That's asking very little.' She tilted her head to him, her grey eyes borrowing some of his own mockery. 'I might have something significant to contribute myself.'

'I hope you have, Natalie. Did you think I was trying to tie you down? Though it would be a source of pleasure to build a house around you. I can just about see you in every room. You have that effect on me.'

'Then I can't write you off as hopeless, now, can I?' For a moment the air was electric between them, and his eyes rested openly on the softly glowing curves of her mouth, a blue shaft of lightning.

'You don't profit by your mistakes, do you?'

'Just a little poke,' she said, her eyes widening.

'And me taking the long way home. Here's Bart, someone who needs me.'

The two men met with the easy camaraderie so difficult to reproduce among women, and Natalie was introduced and responded so charmingly and so intelligently that even Lang smiled on her until such time as he really wanted to get down to essentials and Natalie was given the divine command to precede him into the house of her choice, which just happened to be his own design. At that moment she would rather have liked to have picked on Bruce Duncan's, for instance, for she recognised her father's very elegant style, which hadn't changed a great deal. Bart Hayes' hazel eyes twinkled some sort of message to her and she smiled back at him and walked away to the tree-shaded, stunningly white façade. This house she really liked, and her own brand of professionalism took over, her gaze very clear and assessing, but she couldn't fault him or, would she admit it, approach him. The godlike Lang Frazer! The only trouble was he was a very attractive man.

Inside, the interior made the heart leap with the most exciting spacial feeling, the free flow of space that was a benediction in a hot climate and an added reward for a nation of people who loved to entertain in their homes. The living room level flowed out to the courtyard, open to the hectic blue of the sky, and led away to the window-walled bedrooms on the other side. Natalie, her mind stimulated, began to visualise the inner court as a fine contrast to the rather bold statement of the house and she wondered what plantings and small specimen trees Harry Banks would introduce into the area. With an excellent reputation he should make of it an entrancing private garden retreat.

The soaring walls of the living-dining room were brick, painted white reflecting the abundance of light from the window walls that enclosed the court on three sides. A black wrought iron spiral staircase sprang from the parqueted foyer to a small room, possibly a study, that angled in to the dramatic slant of the roof. All available space had been utilised. It had everything one could wish for —great looks and style, plenty of sunlight and fresh air and in the near future glimpses through the plate glass windows of a green leafy haven.

Natalie's mind's eye was already adorning the floor and the blank walls, placing different pieces of furniture, all sorts of ideas for textural interplay blossoming. Of course there was a budget to consider, and she wondered what the ceiling on that might be. Adrian would have been wild with enthusiasm to accept such a commission, but Adrian, to Natalie's mind, and she liked to think it was an objective opinion, was just that bit casual. She liked to have a plan for herself, a loose one if needs be, but a plan minimised mistakes and mistakes were costly all round.

She crossed the courtyard and slid open the doors leading to the en suite master bedroom. It had the same timber panelling with two-by-four detailing as the ceiling of the main reception rooms of the house. Again stark white walls, the bathroom of generous dimensions decorated with very beautiful Spanish tiles in an arabesque design. Three more bedrooms, smaller in scale, then another bathroom for the younger members of the family, inlaid with equally beautiful tiles in a Wedgwood blue and white scroll but of a less sophisticated design. So far so good; now she had to see the kitchen and the family or second living room.

She was walking determinedly back across the courtyard when Lang Frazer caught up with her, blue eyes blazing with life, his dark hair in the sunlight with unexpected deep copper glints. 'Well?'

'My head is buzzing with ideas!'

'Really!' he said, his voice laden with soft insinuation. 'Now that's an added pleasure!'

'About carpets, drapes, furnishings!' she continued.

'Of course, Natalie. I knew exactly what you meant. How would you go about decorating a place like this?' he asked casually.

'I'd have to discipline all my blossoming ideas first. So many decorative possibilities suggest themselves to me, an endless array of styles would fit in, but once settled it should prove fairly straight-

94

forward, and a great pleasure. I can already feel the pattern of living. I might be in a bit of trouble with a house the size of Maccalla, of course.'

'I'm not talking about Maccalla, Natalie,' he said a shade wearily. 'You have a bit of a fixation there, and Maccalla after all was built as a rich man's mansion. There aren't all that many of them around.'

His blue eyes seemed to be scorching her and she almost shrank from them. 'I'm sorry! I seem to have made you angry.'

'Not at all. If I'm angry it's only at myself. I have a passion for making things over, and with you, Natalie, I'd like to start all over again.'

'You mean I can't be what you want?' She put her head down, conscious of her relative immaturity.

'That's it!' he said with finality, eyes in a bright, blue splash of colour sliding over her. 'Now, let's talk sense. How would you like a job? In brief, making a showcase of this place. I'll have to ensnare you in any way I can.'

'Why, I'd love it!' she said, scared and startled, her whole face illuminated with the idea. 'Opportunities invariably pass right on by if one hesitates.'

'Agreed!' he said dryly, remembering the many times he had jumped in at the deep end.

'And it would be such an achievement. A triumph! A commission from the great Lang Frazer. If I could only pull it off!' Natalie was speaking almost to herself, then she swung about and faced him. 'One thing, am I allowed to do it my way?'

'I'd like to be kept filled in, but yes, you can do it your way. In full measure. As a rule we give these jobs to the proven professionals, but of you I seem to have made any number of exceptions!'

She stared into his face as fixedly as a small cat, her hair velvet black against the gardenia white of her skin. 'Won't I be treading on a few toes?'

'There is that possibility,' he said suavely. 'An impressive collection of toes, actually, but let me worry about that.'

She swung about in an impulsive pirouette, her hair cascading about her enticing young face. 'I can't believe it! How marvellous! Even if my elders and betters are going to gallop in to the attack. I have it now ... totally contemporary, nothing traditional at all. The house has its own stamp on it and I'll stick right along with it. Take the court....'

'Leave it there, little one,' he said, sounding vaguely amused. 'Harry will attend to all that. I promise you he won't let either of us down.'

'What about budgets and things?'

'Get it all down on paper first. I don't expect you to place every stick of furniture to the inch, but give me the basic idea. I assume you work to a plan. Rushing about with great ideas that don't come off spells disaster.'

'You've implied you're prepared to trust me,' she said with young dignity.

'With the decorating, yes, Natalie of the smoky eyes!' There was some shivery odd note in his dark vibrant voice that had the same powerful effect as a caress. The sudden force of her own uprush of feeling almost shocked her. Her small poised head was thrown back, her wide eyes glowing and guarded, strangely secretive.

'Now why are you looking at me like that, Natalie? God knows you're mysterious enough!'

Some part of him she knew was standing well back, curiously detached as though he was sitting in judgment of both of them and very likely her idiotic behaviour. It was with a sense of reprieve that she heard footsteps sounding through the living room behind them, vigour and a great certainty in their steady tap, tap. Both of them turned in that direction to see a tall, very striking woman with short, crackling saffron-coloured curls, on her rakishly thin form a smart very expensive yellow-gold suit with a glorious printed silk blouse beneath. Her accessories were predictably perfect and she had an air of tremendous energy and chic.

'Lang! I was determined to catch you,' she announced in a brittle, clear voice. 'You're so hellishly elusive these days. Another twenty-four hours and I would have had to admit total defeat!'

'Something important?' He moved towards her, speaking almost lightheartedly.

'Not for you, perhaps, darling,' she answered reproachfully. 'For me!'

'What on earth can you mean?'

'Oh, you're dreadful. A dreadful, dreadful man, but so clever!' She came on like a whirlwind, gripping attention, the gold bracelets on her arm jingling. 'Now don't tell me, I know. Drew's daughter! I can see the resemblance. Grace Copeley, dear,' she added, introducing herself and saving time, 'you know, Copeley Associates.'

'How do you do!' said Natalie, politely on cue, accepting the firm, outstretched hand, looking for and not finding a wedding ring.

'Miss, Mrs., what does it matter?' the woman shrugged, accurately reading Natalie's gaze. 'Actually it's Miss, though I have an ex-husband around some place, don't I, Lang?'

'Yes, Gracie!' he said, standing back and smiling at her.

'And don't call me Gracie,' she rounded on him, 'it makes me feel like a period piece, as you very well know!'

'I thought it suited you,' he murmured, his lithe body relaxed.

'Beast! Anyway, darling, what I really want to know and I have to search you up to find out, is, when can I start on this thing? I must say it's all very glorious!'

'Ah, the tricky bit is about to begin!' Lang Frazer snapped out of his negligent pose. 'Actually, Gracie old dear, I've already given one house away.'

'That's news!' She kept the shock out of her voice, but the tiniest little tic caught the edge of her mouth.

'I didn't say it wasn't news!'

'Well, really, darling,' she stared at him, 'you can't blame me if I'm slightly bereft. I mean, we've worked splendidly together in the past.'

'And I'm looking forward to the future, but this house I've given away.'

'But I want it, *damn you*,' she snapped, giving herself away, and spitting the words out through

98

her teeth. Belatedly she turned to Natalie. 'Forgive me, Miss Calvert, I normally adhere to good manners, but this man ...! God! Sometimes I just want to scream out loud.'

'Scream if you like!' Lang said idly. 'It worked wonders last time!'

'If you'll excuse me,' said Natalie, trying to be helpful, 'I'll go and curl up quietly in a corner.'

'No deal. Just stay where you are. Actually, Gracie, it's to Natalie here that I've given the job.'

'Why, how odd! How terribly, terribly odd!' Grace Copeley turned on the girl with inexhaustible critical facilities, not particularly relishing what she saw. 'Have you come straight from art school, then, the Technical College? Speak up, dear, don't be nervous!'

'Honestly, Miss Copeley,' Natalie said gently, 'I haven't stolen or cheated for the job. I've been working for a few years now with a wonderful firm, full of wonderful, wonderful people!' she added a trace maliciously, for Miss Copeley favoured the double adjective. 'Courtland and Mason.'

'Never heard of them!' Grace Copeley said savagely, when she *had*. 'What am I to deduce from this, Lang? Play ball or else?'

'Why take it like that, darling?' he asked in a voice he kept for the sweet and defenceless. 'Choose any other house you like. Any house at all.'

'But *this* one!'

'That's right!'

Her disappointment was so acute, the tiny little tic so much in evidence, Natalie began to feel distinctly guilty, as if she had run off with an ill-deserved prize. There was an acid look in Grace Copeley's green eyes.

'I don't mind telling you, Miss Calvert, I hope you go on your....'

'*Gracie!*'

'... neck! You swine, Lang!'

'So nice of you to drop over and tell me.' His face was alive with enormous verve, his blue eyes held Grace Copeley's. 'How about dinner tomorrow night?'

'To salve your conscience?' she said bitterly. 'All right, then, that sounds fine. Eight, at my place?'

'I'm pretty good, Miss Copeley,' Natalie said tepidly as though she was obliged to defend herself.

'You'd better be, kid,' the other woman said shortly, 'because you know my views on the subject. I'll be one step behind you ready to take over at a moment's notice.'

'The real trouble with you, Gracie,' Lang Frazer drawled, 'is you're business, business, business!'

'You fool!' Grace Copeley suddenly whirled, a tall woman, strength in her long hands, and kissed him hard on the mouth. It was as plain as her very fine straight nose that she found him outrageously, frantically attractive, and Natalie didn't blame her for one moment but rather applauded her initiative. Lang Frazer would tantalise at least ten women a day, but very few of them would be capable of such direct action. One wondered how her husband got away, or very likely he was pushed out of the inner sanctum. A lot of women would be afraid of her. A lot of men too, for Grace Copeley looked what she was, a clever successful woman with superb taste. A kind of ruthlessness was possessing her now and she grasped Lang Frazer's arm, not the least averse to bossing him. 'I'm taking this man off for a few minutes—and just try to stop me!'

'Such a thought never crossed my mind!' Natalie said. *Were such a thing possible.*

'Goodbye, then!' Grace Copeley tacked on with mingled pity and scorn, not attempting to conceal her own upset. 'I'd like to say I've got a great deal of faith in you, but that would be telling a lie. I just thought I'd mention it.'

'My faith in myself isn't exactly on the weak side,' Natalie informed her.

'My dear!' Frost dripped off the green glance. 'It's just not possible you're as capable as I, and there's still time to reverse this brute's decision.'

'Of sheer necessity only, Gracie. I've checked Natalie out, and she's her father's daughter, let's face it. *Quality.* Don't glower,' Lang chided her, 'it completely destroys your attractiveness!'

'What the hell else do you expect me to do?'

'As a matter of fact. . . .' He almost pushed her through the sliding glass panels and the rest of it was lost to Natalie, who had gone a little white with a concentration of guilt. It was a good twenty minutes later before she caught sight of Lang putting Grace Copeley into her car, like the Machiavelli he was, leaning forward to kiss the stoically turned cheek. Natalie, peering through the kitchen windows despite her conviction that she had been well brought up, saw that green razor sharp glance melt to a look of appeal. She turned away quickly, having to imagine the rest. Her own emotions were becoming more purified by the minute, more impersonal, as she realised she was by no means the only woman who fired at Lang Frazer's touch. Right at this moment she felt incapable of exchanging another word with him. It was a curious mood and she didn't dare analyse the cause for it.

Of course he noticed the change in her, being well versed in the ways of women, but he wisely made no comment. He simply showed her over the rest of the estate and Natalie very determinedly didn't allow him to distract her in any way.

'Do you still want to have lunch with me?' he inquired dryly as they walked back to the car. Her heart gave a little involuntary skip and she answered, feeling martyred:

'Perhaps another day?'

'You *don't* want to?' he tilted her chin with long, hurting fingers and made her look at him, her eyes wide and darkening with unsatisfactory, conflicting emotions. Some piercing current passed between them and she drew in her breath sharply, wanting to clutch him.

'You'll come,' he said, deciding the matter.

Afterwards Natalie wished that she hadn't, for the rest of the day had the peculiar intimacy of a dream. An awareness on both sides that each sought to hide but neither had any difficulty in seeing. Lang could so easily hurt her, and that, Natalie was painfully discovering, was highly significant. If he sometimes saw in the clear shining depths of her eyes that she was silently imploring his help he was very slow to offer it, something in his manner subtly enhancing the perilous feeling she had of a dangerous affinity. Even their spirit had an odd harmony, the things that they liked and the things that they talked about, so late that night, tossing fretfully, Natalie decided she had gone through a strange experience that afternoon in the form of an hypnotic trance. When she finally did drift into sleep it was to dream that she was hurling headlong from a fleecy white cloud pinnacle through the vivid blue sky into Lang Frazer's waiting arms.

CHAPTER FOUR

Natalie slept late in the morning and when she came down to breakfast she was dismayed to find Britt riveted to the table like an automaton programmed to stir tea.

'Good morning!' Even to Natalie's own ears it sounded like a nervous prayer.

'Nothing could persuade me it's *that*!' Britt's voice settled it, so frozen the words splintered in a heap on the ground.

'Oh?' Natalie poured herself coffee, startled by the reflection of her own face in the mirrored credenza, very pale within the massy black curtain of hair. 'Anything wrong?' She turned away and sat a respectful distance down the table, still determined to hold her own.

'I had a phone call from a friend of mine—Grace Copeley,' Britt said as though it explained all.

'She didn't lose any time,' commented Natalie.

'No!' For all the brilliant, glittery sunlight that spilled into the morning room, Britt had a frighteningly pinched look. 'What I *don't* know is how you persuaded Lang to allow you to attempt such a thing.'

'The project house, you mean?' Natalie asked carefully, finding the perfectly good coffee as bitter as gall.

'Don't waste my time and yours,' Britt said unpleasantly. 'I'm exhausted enough already just thinking about it. Grace is furious and ready to spill her fury all over town.'

'I don't think so. She was mad enough, certainly, but I don't think she's a vindictive woman.' *Like you*, Natalie added silently, extraordinarily vicious and mean when you're cornered.

'For Lang to be such a fool! I can't believe it. In fact nothing is easy for me these days. Not with you in the house again, determined to undermine me at every turn. It's no wonderful frolic for me to sit back and take second place, but I have to submit to this new arrangement for your father's sake.' Britt looked up briefly and her amber eyes were haunted by the spectre of utter failure. 'I never wished to have to take you into account again,' she said in a voice that made Natalie want to take shelter. Her pleasure in the bright morning died.

'I wondered how long it would take you to say that,' she murmured almost absently, starting to shake inside. 'I've been home how long? Six weeks? I suppose you've been hoarding that up.'

Britt's face twisted into an odd smile. '*I* know and *you* know that nothing has ever been resolved between us. I blame you bitterly for the loss of my child.'

'Are you sure you were able to distinguish between fantasy and fact? Like some mad queen frightened of being deposed. I believe you were pregnant with a phantom child—the new heir and an ideal ignominious way of seeing me banished.'

'I *was* pregnant!' Britt maintained, her face in the naked morning so malevolent that Natalie

105

visibly recoiled when she thought she wouldn't turn a hair. Five years in the wilderness hadn't made her a lot stronger after all.

'If you keep this up, Britt,' she said quietly, 'you'll make life unbearable for all of us.'

'It will be enough for me if I can make it unbearable for you in a thousand small ways!'

'And you really mean it. It's beyond all reason. Please stop now before this whole scene becomes thoroughly ugly and uncivilised.'

Britt's brittle laugh came as a shock. 'You and your *uncivilised*!' she sneered. 'Your father is the same way—always the civilised gentleman living in easy splendour. Hates scenes, the aristocrat.'

'While you seem to like railing like a fishwife.'

There was a stunned silence with the echo of Natalie's voice ringing in it and Britt cried out, genuinely shocked, 'How wicked of you to speak to me like that!'

Natalie could have laughed at the irony of it, but she was seized by the same old sick sensation that Britt always induced in her. Britt's gleaming tawny head was thrown back, her wide mouth quivering.

'You're heading for a breakdown,' Natalie observed.

'A remarkably astute analysis!'

'I thought you were on valium, but I think it's something else,' Natalie said slowly. 'Your *eyes*!'

For the length of a second Britt's unwinking gaze glittered, then fell. She was a neurotic woman, easy prey to all sorts of dangerous fixations. 'Now Grace,' she said, abruptly changing the subject and becoming confident again, 'Grace Copeley is a very clever woman and very ambitious and she has a message to be delivered to you. There's nothing you could possibly teach her about anything. She has something little girls like you lack and she's a pretty smooth operator. It may disturb you to know she has true determination, and I can risk telling you she wants Lang. Both of us can see you've got a pretty face, though the sight of you sets my teeth together. Pretty faces can cause sudden infatuations that just as suddenly fade out. Lang for all his brilliance at his profession is a man like other men, temporarily susceptible, and this ... this aberration to my mind proves it. If you're something of a novelty to him now he'll soon weary of your big eyes as he has done many times in the past, and to help him along I'll speak to him.'

'And that, I hope, will get you precisely nowhere,' Natalie said with irony. 'Lang Frazer would go his own way as a kind of natural law and his professional mind is as brilliant as a diamond and just as hard. That he would be influenced by a pretty face in that respect is the most preposterous suggestion. I'm good at my job. Not as experienced as Miss Copeley, of course, but I can succeed without any double or triple dealing. Besides, there couldn't be anything new about me you could tell him.'

'As luck would have it, no. You may be able to put one across Grace, but never me. I won't have you hanging about like some dreadful *doppelganger*. I want you out. Mark that down in your memory—and don't be foolish enough to think I won't find a way.'

'Yes, you're big on accidents!' Natalie suggested,

her own temper rising, more than ever certain Britt had always been lying. 'What is it you think I'll wrest from you? What's the prize? It's not Father—you've lost all interest in him. I'm not such a fool I can't see that.'

'And it's no discovery!' Britt almost shouted, her voice ugly. 'It's Maccalla I want. One day this house will acknowledge me, though it doesn't heed me yet!'

'Forgive me if I think you're a trifle mad. You speak as if the house had a living presence.'

'So it has!' Britt said in an amazing volte-face that was twice as chilling as her icy hostility. Her face went slack and seemed to collapse. 'It mocks me!' she went on with a terrible look of rage and despair. 'Alive with laughter. Your mother and that witch of a grandmother you had. *Lady* Sabien —bah! That one, what trouble she made!'

'If you're thinking along those lines then I should begin pitying you,' said Natalie, her own nerves tightening.

'Pity yourself, dear,' Britt whispered, spinning right back on course again, the mad seesaw of bristling manias. 'You and I are locked in a mortal crisis. Don't deceive yourself. What you see in my face is really there. I hate you and I want Maccalla *afterwards*. Marrying your father was difficult enough in the first place, my only triumph up until that date. I loved him then. He was everything I wanted—but now he's burned out. What else is left but the house? A century wouldn't be too long to wait for it.'

Natalie watched her stepmother's pale gloating

face, expressionless. 'One should beware of wanting things, Britt. Maccalla belongs to my father, and my father is very much alive.'

'If I thought *you* were dead, I could be almost happy.'

'God forgive you for saying it! Such hate is beyond all explaining and it will poison you yet. This is going to go hard on you, Britt, but this time I'm not going. I'm going to put up a fight!' Such zealous conviction was in Natalie's clear young voice, Britt dropped her frightening stare. If Natalie expected the end whiplash of her step-mother's tongue, Britt's tirade was spent. The light of battle left the long golden eyes and she bowed her tawny head into her hands and burst into a storm of weeping—a sickening, hysterical sound with a dangerous imbalance.

It was Janet Hood who caught the hoarse, choking sound of it and came quickly into the morning room, her quick eyes sizing up the situation. Natalie stood like a small drained ghost of herself, her face paper-white.

'I beg your pardon, but I couldn't help hearing. Mrs. Calvert, isn't she well?'

Natalie turned her head rather vaguely, looking so young and stricken Janet was roused to anger. She well knew the climate of the house. She went around the table, speaking directly to Britt. 'Mrs. Calvert, can I help you?'

At the sound of her voice, Britt threw up her head, the wetness of tears grotesquely smearing her mascara. 'For heaven's sake, get out!' she shouted. 'How dare you burst in like this? Who wants you?

I'm hiding behind no pretty veil for you, Nurse. You don't mean a damned thing to me one way or the other. *Get out!* You'll get no pseudo-Calvert charm from me!'

Janet felt repelled, but her eyes didn't waver. 'It would be a good idea if you stopped this sort of thing at once,' she said quietly.

'Why?' Britt challenged her, her voice ugly. 'You must be used to family conflicts. Besides, it's most amusing to be told what to do in one's own home and by a simple nurse.'

'A nurse, yes, but simple, *no*,' Janet retorted austerely, with formidable, down-beating eyes. 'Mr. Calvert will be downstairs in a few minutes, and I remind you that I hold his wellbeing above everything else.'

'Oh, spare me the long bravura!' Britt almost groaned. She threw up a shapely bejewelled hand and the diamonds winked blue fire. 'I find the ideals of your lofty profession quite boring.'

Janet stood back, seeing quite clearly the dark aura that pulsed around Britt's head, a curious reddish black. Sometimes, she thought dismally, the second sight was distinctly unnerving, considering Mrs. Calvert was already exhibiting a few blatant symptoms of running downhill. Why should she complicate things so unnecessarily when pretty nearly everyone in a sick person's household was only too anxious to do the right thing? Natalie, poor child, swayed like a pale wraith, and Janet leaned over and pushed the girl into a chair.

'Sit down, child. You're as white as a sheet.'

'A full mustering, how nice!' Britt laughed with

biting sarcasm. 'The dutiful daughter and the nurse, a coalition formed against me—but you won't win. I've never trusted you, Nurse, and this doesn't concern you, so don't make it your life's work. You'll be out of here before you know it, but let Drew come down by all means and find us in a huddle.'

'And that he *won't* do!' Janet spun around in a burst of decisive action, such contempt in her eyes that she actually got the younger woman to her feet, as though she feared physical reprisal.

'I'm up, Nurse,' Britt said brightly, turning sharply white as though she was about to faint. 'Just like that. You looked quite the avenging angel, and I've always had a fanciful imagination. Your timely intervention has won out. I suppose you've had a lifetime of nosing about at other people's keyholes. No, don't come near me. *I* don't require your services. You revolt me. I'm perfectly capable of walking out of here by myself.'

Despite herself Janet found herself shuddering. In her entire nursing career she had never met another woman such as Mrs. Britt Calvert. Looking her best she was a very glamorous woman, but she was extraordinarily vindictive when the longer one lived one realised life has a way of paying us out in our own coin. What Britt Calvert's future would be Janet didn't know, but there could be no peace of mind there.

'What an atrocious way to start the day!' she found herself murmuring. Outside the vast expanse of window wall, roses were blossoming amid their dark green foliage—the new beauty, Princess

Margaret, fragrant, bright pink and prolifically free flowering; Janet's own favourite, Queen Elizabeth, with its china pink clusters. All the roses were arranged in long beds of the same colour, Ophelia and Prima Ballerina and the luminous pale pink of Royal Highness. Incredible to think that inside the wall the pervading climate was hostility.

Natalie came to stand at her side, and the two of them looked out over the flaunting summer beauty of the garden.

'I'm sorry about that, Janet. You must know now that my stepmother hates me.'

'She sounded plain ordinary jealous to me,' Janet said, trying to reduce the bald truth of it. 'Undoubtedly she's under a great strain. You'd best keep out of her way.'

'I thought I was doing that,' Natalie said wryly.

'I know! The thing is, my dear, although your father is making wonderful progress, I for one wouldn't dare upset him. Then all our hard work, all our sacrifices would count for nothing.'

'I'll never upset him again, Janet,' Natalie said fervently. 'I'll put up with anything.' Her limpid grey eyes were over-bright and distressed. 'Britt thinks I'm after Maccalla.'

'One slip of a girl!' Janet said lightly, deciding to tread water. Maccalla, she knew, would fetch a fortune if sold up, and that was not counting the exquisite and dazzling accumulation of the finest eighteenth and nineteenth-century furnishings and antiques, the paintings, the silver and the porcelains, the countless ornaments, the ivory, the Dresden, Limoges, and Cloisonné ware. The house was as fascinating as a museum with generations of collectors and much of it inherited from the Calvert family home in England. There was very little she could say there, and money, an abundance of it or too little, invariably spelt trouble. 'A big house like this,' she continued thoughtfully, 'is meant for a large family, lots of children about, though I suppose not many people could afford its upkeep. Then too all the treasures would have to be locked up.'

'They never were for me,' Natalie said, and smiled for the first time, brightening. 'I adore Maccalla. It's the most romantic house and it made my childhood so much the richer. The fantasies I used to weave for myself! I think it's given me a great sense of beauty, grace and symmetry and history too. I suppose one could even say it represents a way of life that has actually passed—the age of elegance. Now it's the space age, advanced technology and the strictly functional, but the lure of beauty must still attract the creative artist. How to exploit the two images at once. I love Maccalla, but I'm not mercenary. I haven't come back to claim my inheritance. All I want is for my father to be well again. He owes me nothing. It's all the other way about!'

'I know, dear,' Janet said quickly, moved to compassion. 'So why upset yourself?'

'Because the sad truth is, Janet, and I'm obliged to accept it, Britt won't rest until I'm out of this house.'

'Very likely. Perhaps when your father is well again, really well, I mean, it would be best if you did move to a place of your own not too far away. A beautiful girl like you, with your own vision, should have the world at her feet.'

'What is it, Janet, about Father?' Natalie asked, her gaze very soft and clear in her camellia face. 'You sound as if you have qualms about him. If you have, please tell me.'

'I just don't want him upset,' Janet explained. 'So that means you must be a good brave girl and take all the punishment your stepmother is prepared to dish out, at least for a little while.'

'And what about you? It can't be pleasant for you having to swallow Britt's insults.'

'Don't you worry about me, dear. I'm an old stager at turning a deaf ear. I'm committed to getting your father strong on his feet again.'

'And that's it, isn't it, Janet? Commitment. Determination to see a thing through. You're a career woman.'

'Ever since I was a little girl!' Janet declared, not following the trend of Natalie's thought. 'My father was a country doctor, you see, dedicated. He died poor but worshipped from near and afar. My mother wasn't in the profession, but she too nursed every lame duck for miles around. You might say I was a natural.'

'And how fortunate for us! You've been very good for Father.'

'I hope so. Now what about some fresh coffee?' Janet asked. 'I'll go and get it, me being the efficient one.'

'What an excellent idea. I haven't had anything —not that I really want it now. I don't get along too

114

well with Vera in any case. You will have a cup with me?'

'I'll do that.'

'Fine. I've some news for you. Pleasant this time.'

'I'm looking forward to that,' Janet called over her shoulder.

Later, seated in serene isolation out on the veranda, they sipped at their fragrant coffee, with a scoop of fresh cream and a dash of cinnamon. 'Here's to peace!' Natalie said with a wry smile.

'Now that's a nice sentiment. I'll drink to that.'

Almost on cue, quite theatrically, Britt swept out on to the veranda, very stylishly dressed, her make-up perfect but the skin stretched taut over her high cheekbones. 'I'm going out!' she said with extreme sarcasm. 'I'm sure you can all manage without me for a while.' Then she was walking out towards the portico on her way to the old stables converted into a multiple garage.

Alleluia! thought Janet in silent acknowledgment. Exit Lady Macbeth.

In a house the size of Maccalla, Natalie found she had to retreat to the original Calvert cottage in the garden as the only safe place to protect and encourage the spontaneity of her ideas. With all her concentration needed to realise her commission she reasoned that the best way to achieve this was scrupulously to avoid all confrontations with Britt. It was exile again, but what a difference, for she was wonderfully busy and absorbed in doing something she did extremely well, being naturally inventive with an inbuilt ability for solving decorative problems.

When she first told her father about her commission, it had been almost impossible for him to continue normal conversation, so ludicrously surprised had he been. Had she told him she was dancing Giselle with the Bolshoi Ballet he would have taken it equally well, but Lang came to her rescue in some private conversation, vouching for her ability on the strength, as she imagined, of what she had accomplished with her own home unit. He had, in fact, omitted to tell her of a long encouraging conversation he had with her old firm which proved highly insignificant in the long run. After that it was plain sailing, with her father proud and anxious that she should successfully carry off such a coup. It was he who suggested 'the old cottage' which had long since been transformed into a dream guest house, entirely self-contained. As well it was wonderfully cool in the summer, sheltered by magnificent old shade trees, and it offered magical, serene glimpses of the swans sailing over the lake. With her father looking happy and enthusiastic and Lang smiling sardonically indulgent upon her, Natalie thought herself in heaven. All that was left was for her imaginative statements to develop into reality.

Whole days went by scouting around the showrooms and decorator shops, making careful on-site planning of details, then Natalie removed herself to the cottage until such time as the master plan and overall design was submitted to her father and Lang for possible editing. She rose very early and went to bed late, going over and over the details until her plans seemed as perfect and comprehensive on paper as she could make them. Of necessity, the furniture and accessories had to be moderately priced, but there was plenty of well put together modern furniture about and she counted on using the countless items of non-furniture, the cubes and the fitments and the stacked multi-purpose units to hold books and objects, sound equipment and the hideous, glaring eye of the T.V.

She had started at the beginning, visualising her clients, the eventual owners of the house, and she dealt in her imagination with them. The young marrieds, contemporary-orientated, two young children, a boy and a girl, allowing her to decorate a bedroom for each. Her clients had listed their requirements, which included a flexible master plan, comfort and value and a bit of excitement thrown in. She longed to place one really good piece of quality furniture, for her own preference, antique, but she would have to ask Lang about that, In the end she came up with a decor that had young and assured elegance all over it. It was such a pleasure to work with the continuous flowing spaces Lang had sculpted. It was not Maccalla with its noble proportions and exquisite architectural embellishments standing foursquare under its tower, obeying all the rules of perspective, massing and symmetry with its splendid portico. This was a house totally today that would look good tomorrow —severe in comparison, a striking white shell, with its stained timber outrigging and brilliant expanses of glass, drawing strength to itself in its very lack of ornamentation. Natalie liked to think of it as a starkly pristine jewel box that she could make glow from within, a combination of the sheer force of the architect's personality projected into his creation and her own ambiance which had, had she known it, immense fascination. The house was to be an expression of both their personalities, and this knowledge she hugged to herself like a child.

It was out at the site that she first met Bruce Duncan, who had been kept hard at his job like a small boy with homework. Bruce was very attractive, brown-haired, brown-eyed, very tall and still a little gangly, a lively, latter-day Anthony Perkins, and a fast mover, for the same night he invited Natalie 'to the theatre, to the flicks, dinner, you name it!' and a party the following Saturday night.

With a mind satiated with furnishings and floor coverings and drapes, Natalie was only too pleased to accept his artistically delivered invitation. Bruce, as he was quick to inform her, had followed her deliberately to the site from Maccalla where he had been paying a courtesy visit to her father, advantageously using his time to try and extract a bit of valuable information of a particular stress problem Drew Calvert was strong on. Unfortunately 'the Boss' had simply not realised which way Bruce's infinitely crafty enquiries were heading, being too busy singing Lang's praises, 'the Man of Destiny' and the hidden abilities of his only child. The only information Bruce had been able to ascertain was that Natalie had gone out to the Bellwood estate that morning. There he had trapped her. As he put it himself, guerrilla tactics. It was simply not possible to compare or contrast him with Lang, in fact

Bruce begged her not to do this, but Natalie liked him all the same. It was a mutual affair.

That evening she dressed with relaxed confidence for dinner at Gallio's where the *haute cuisine* was carried to extraordinary lengths but well worth the unheard-of prices. The dance floor and the four-piece group was very good as well for those who didn't excel at intimate tête-à-tête conversation. Natalie and Bruce were good at both, dancing, talking, laughing as they did from the moment Bruce insisted on ordering a Chateau Lafitte Rothschild of the year she was born. The sommelier ignored him, that particular wine being in the vicinity of a thousand dollars a case, and suggested an excellent Barossa Valley dry red or a slightly chilled Beaujolais if Bruce considered domestic wine just that bit vulgar.

'And fancy a waiter trying to upstage me!' grinned Bruce when the sommelier had gone. 'Let me adjust that shade for my dazzled eyes. You're beautiful, Natalie—unbelievably. Crystal eyes, pearly skin, and hair as black and shiny as a crow's wing. From the way Lang has been so very reticent about you I rather suspected he was too kind to mention that you were terribly plain. Not that your father could have a plain daughter, and how glad I am to see him so much more his old self again. We're very fond of Drew, you know, and I for one am not ashamed to use those very words. He's a fine man, a good man, brilliant but very approachable. Like Lang. Funny, that! The not so brilliant ones are the ones to look out for, snobbish and exalted as hell. What do you think of Lang?'

he shot at her.

'He did give me my job and he did bring me home again,' Natalie said carefully, looking at that moment very enchanting and mysterious.

'Lang has influence everywhere. The Man of Destiny, we call him in the business, as I think I told you. But that's not what I mean. It's also commonly known he's the great enchanter so far as women are concerned—handsome, well integrated, incredibly sexy. Don't you think so?'

'I hadn't really noticed.'

'Oh, come on now, Natalie, I thought women had their own radar about such things. I mean, Lang's physical appeal is just an extension of his mind. I mean, he's brilliant—the only way to describe him, and he's an enormous influence on me. My own work has improved out of sight. I think I'm really beginning to develop as an architect.'

'You're very modest, Bruce. Lang told me himself you're very talented.'

'Oh, darling, that's it. Talented. I want to be fantastic, and Lang's the key. The way that man can adapt designs to their surroundings! A lot of the big boys are as jealous as hell of him. He doesn't incite any neutral passions, so don't pass me off with "you haven't noticed".'

'I know he put Grace Copeley's nose out of joint, picking me.'

'Ah, Grace!' Bruce said with an odd note in his voice. 'I can't actually say Grace grabs me. She likes to give advice, and tell me a worse companion than a woman who likes to give advice. Now you it would take very little effort to be absolutely wild about, but Grace, no. She's madly in love with Lang, and it's no confidence I'm revealing, because she tells everyone. Hot-shot career women aren't my line in any case.'

'And why is that?' she asked dryly. These men with their line!

'Because, darling girl—and don't curl that pretty, ardent mouth at me—there's one fatal flaw in them, they've lost all their seductive ways. Grace is a very striking woman. I mean, she's a terrific dresser and she has great style, but she's too pushy. She'd get just as far not trying so hard. Pushy women destroy the feminine ambiance. I like to bask in it—like now.'

'Really?'

'Yes. I used to think a blonde in a black dress was the sexiest thing there was, but now I'm not at all sure. You have very dazzling skin.'

'Thank you, Bruce.' Natalie looked into his brown, intrigued eyes. 'But I think you've conjured up someone. No, *two* people, more a party. Don't turn round. It's Grace Copeley and Lang.'

Over Bruce's finely tailored shoulders Natalie met a gaze with all the compelling brilliance of blue ice. There were a lot of attractive men around. She was dining with one, yet Lang seemed to have a very enviable edge on the lot of them. As though he couldn't conceal his own power, or indeed wasn't particularly aware of it. *The great enchanter*, she thought, and smiled at him, an elegant, mysterious little motion of her mouth.

'Don't you do that!' Bruce said so abruptly she almost jumped.

'What?'

'Make eyes at Lang like that. You're with me, remember?'

'And I'd much rather be here than there,' she said truthfully as Grace Copeley picked up the direction of Lang's gaze. She made a little scale-like exercise with her fingers and they had to be content with that. Lang lifted a hand to them and Bruce sprang to his feet and bowed, earning an appreciative very white smile. Then the head waiter was upon the whole group, the élite by the look of them, and Natalie transferred her total attention back to Bruce.

'She's an awful bitch, Grace!' Bruce muttered, obviously rattled by something.

'She looks more like a dahlia on a stalk,' Natalie commented fairly. 'That's a super dress.'

'She'd swop places with you any day, duckie. You're the most eye-catching woman in this room. It's great for my ego.'

'You're not bad for mine, either!'

They continued to treat one another extravagantly right through the meal, laughing a great deal with not one risqué word spoken. Just two vital, attractive young people who could communicate without spelling it all out.

About ten o'clock, Lang wandered over to their table, perfect in every detail. 'Hello, you two! I just thought I'd come over and pay you a call, not that either of you look as though you need any stimulus.' His very blue eyes with their thick black webbing of lashes studied both young faces with impartial affection. 'Sit down, Bruce. You always make me feel like a professor.'

'Well, it's true I hang on your every word,' Bruce said, notably serious.

'And *now* you know "Natalie"'s not ugly. How are you, Natalie?'

'Enjoying myself, Lang,' she said, smiling at the Russian accent.

'How's the master plan going?'

'Wonderfully well. *I hope*,' she tacked on, and gave a little gurgle in her throat. 'It should be ready for editing in a day or so.'

'Do you actually want that badly to be a career girl?' Bruce asked. 'I say, Lang, Gracie's looking very slightly irked.'

'Really? Then I can't upset her. Before the night's over, Natalie, I'm coming back to ask for a dance. You don't mind, Bruce?' Lang asked suavely.

'It would do me no good to say yes?'

'Not in the least. Junior partners are obliged to accept these things. Natalie, did I tell you you look as mysteriously elegant as a blue Persian?' Lang stood up and looked down at her with an amused, dangerous face.

'Don't try and take my girl over!' Bruce warned halfheartedly, a young man who was determined to improve himself at every turn. Right now he was preoccupied with watching Lang Frazer's effect on women. If he watched close enough he might pick up a few things that might be useful. The trouble was he didn't look like Lang, although he had found out the name of his tailor, he didn't talk like Lang, though he had no Australian drawl, or not much of a one anyway, and he didn't have Lang's ability, nor would he ever have, and no sense in pretending.

'All right, I surrender!' Natalie smiled into those vivid blue eyes.

'What an odd thing to say!' Bruce looked from one to the other.

'Lang likes getting his own way,' Natalie informed him. 'Haven't you noticed?'

'Indeed I have, but he's a straight shooter.'

'It seems, Lang,' she said dryly, 'you charm everyone.'

'Gracie at any rate. I'll see you later.'

'Now that's one of the few truly foolish things I've ever agreed to,' Bruce began to mourn, looking after Lang's tall, lean figure. 'It might be safer to leave now.'

'Not at all, I'm having a lovely time, thanks to you, Bruce. May I have a glass of champagne?'

'As long as we're celebrating *our* meeting.'

'What else, naturally!'

'Then the answer is yes,' Bruce swivelled his head slightly to attract the attention of the waiter, whose attitude had mellowed towards him, at the same time risking a sweeping, comprehensive glance over Lang's super-sophisticated group. 'Be that as it may,' he said almost to himself, 'a lot of things aren't right at Lang's table.'

'Whatever are you talking about?' she queried.

'Ah! It's all right, dear, Grace's expression is improving. I detest jealous women, don't you?'

'Jealous men, too,' said Natalie, her forehead crinkling.

'And I bet you've come across many.'

'A few. While the waiter brings out the champagne let's dance, shall we?'

'I'm breathless at the thought of it, in fact, I'm trembling inside,' Bruce declared, which was nothing short of the truth.

Half an hour after, Lang's party broke up and he and Grace came over to join the younger couple. It very plainly wasn't Grace's idea, but she was gaining on her initial reluctance, turning a worldly conniving face on them, waving. Lang, Grace had found, she just could not manage, which was disconcerting and odd when she had left her husband for the very opposite reason.

Natalie and Bruce watched their progress in a semi-expectant silence, each thinking their own thoughts, which were in no way similar, until finally Bruce whispered just above his breath:

'It takes a lot more than a beautiful dress to make a beautiful woman. Of course she's very glamorous and she knows everybody ... power-mad!'

'Ssh!' urged Natalie, fearful he would be overheard.

'Don't *ssh* me, pretty one!'

'They're coming, or rather our sommelier is.' The head waiter beat him to it, forging ahead to the table and placing extra chairs most carefully for the approaching couple. He was rewarded with a smile in addition to the generous tip.

Natalie fell to admiring the dress. It was really something on Grace's racy frame, her extreme thinness making the sensational plunge of the neck acceptable—over dinner, at any rate. It was couture, obviously, and ultra-sophisticated, in the most beautiful gold satin. With it Grace wore a long rope of what appeared to be, from their remarkable soft lustre, real pearls. A Persian gold glitter jacket went with it, adorned with tiny seed pearls. So far Grace had not put it on. Natalie let her gaze wander on. A foot behind Grace, Lang looked the big wheel wherever he went, elegant, powerful, faintly satirical. Together they looked magnetic, turning the most hardened heads.

When they finally reached the table Lang bowed with elaborate grace. 'May we join you?' he asked. 'And do *not* try to stop us.'

'Good evening!' Grace contributed by way of an overture and a flicker of something that appeared like malice. Lang's dark well shaped head was near her saffron-coloured hair as he adjusted her chair and arranged her beautiful jacket over the back of the seat.

'I say, Grace,' Bruce offered gallantly, 'you look sumptuous tonight. The pearls, are they real, dear?'

'What do you think?' Grace retorted without a blink, giving Natalie's seductive young black a good going over. 'How are you, Miss Calvert?'

'Natalie, *please*,' Natalie smiled. 'Don't let's be public enemies!'

'Girls!' Lang looked from one to the other with a tiny flick of remonstration towards Natalie. 'Now, what are we drinking?'

'No more for me,' Grace declared with a strong shudder. 'I fear and dread the ravages of alcohol.'

'Then what?' Lang looked at her with a sidelong, definitely exciting glance that just could have been cruel, but Natalie couldn't be sure. So far he had barely glanced at her.

'Talk!' Grace supplied brightly. 'Talk. Talk. Talk. Lots of happy talk.'

'Did you hear that, Bruce?' Lang glanced at his junior colleague. 'You've had your time organised. Natalie, would you be kind to me and just dance? Any more talk today and I'll blow my mind!'

'Kick off, Grace!' said Bruce, getting well into stride. 'Shoot from the hip. What's new at Copeley's? I hear you have a wonderful way with curtains.'

'You cheeky little upstart!' said Grace.

'He admires you, Gracie, can't you tell? Catch up with the news while Natalie and I dance.'

With a disturbing presence at her back, Natalie allowed herself to be steered on to the dance floor.

'A big night?' Lang asked, turning her into his arms.

'I like Bruce very much,' she said, nearly but not quite forgetting Bruce's existence.

'Is that the answer I asked for? Actually, for the record, I like Bruce too. *And* he moves with top speed. I didn't even know you had met.'

'Yes, this morning!' Natalie supplied, eyes downbent, in a giddy, decidedly sensuous state. Did he know it?

His hand on her bare arm tightened. 'Just what I said. Full speed ahead—and I'm not sure that I'm pleased about it either!' He caught her closer into his arms and she stumbled a little.

'Mark that down to the champagne,' she said, daring a brief glance.

'Natalie, Natalie!' He relaxed all of a sudden, his voice slowed to the softest drawl. 'You're absolutely delicious to a bone-weary, overworked architect. God, how I've missed your father! Don't let's talk. I just want to capture the feel of you, the scent of you. After a day of infighting I find I desperately need you.'

'You were giving a great performance of needing Grace an hour ago. In fact, you looked a winning combination.'

'How impolite of you to mention that now.' He drew back a little and looked down into her face. Natalie could feel the colour come up under her skin. If he didn't stop looking at her in that particular way she would be shattered, like so much glass, very fragile. His eyes were the same limitless blue of the sky or the ocean, and this excitement he was engendering between them could very easily be a mirage. Fire ran through her at his touch and there was nothing she could do at this moment to make it go away.

'Natalie, you're trembling,' he said.

'I always do in the face of danger.'

'I can't credit you're meaning me.'

'I can't explain it either,' she said, a little shakily. 'A different game. Different players, perhaps?'

'Don't talk like that.'

'I can make you angry, can't I?' she asked.

'Yes. You're one of the femmes fatales of this world. Your face tells all. Your smile. *Smile* at me, Natalie. Not all those bittersweet little glances. Thank God, Bruce and Grace are hitting it off like soulmates. That's the good part about Bruce, he's reliable!'

And you're dynamite! Natalie thought, going beyond reasoning, just moving, feeling.... Lang too fell silent and he touched her thudding pulse. Then, for no good reason, he lifted her wrist and kissed the fine sensitive skin and the fragile blue vein.

He frightened her! She could love him—the thought rose up to meet her like a great cloud, and how, oh, how was she going to cure herself? It would be unthinkable to love Lang Frazer, shattering. But she believed at that moment she did. Certainly he was coming to haunt her. She drew away from him a little. Away from the impossible!

'No!' His soft denial registered the effect of her femininity on him. 'You're not going anywhere, Natalie. I want you all to myself.'

'I don't count!' she said, and foolishly her eyes shimmered with tears.

'What a stupid thing to say, Natalie, and you're not stupid at all. Don't make waves, little one. Not tonight, *please*. I'm practically begging you, and it's not a thing I do often. Besides, it's already too late!'

He caught a blue-lustred strand of her hair and twined it around his finger. 'You haven't changed a bit since that portrait was done of you and your mother. *"Nadia, Natalie."* It's very memorable!'

'I thought you hadn't seen it,' she said, a catch to her voice.

'Neither I had until the other day. Your father told me where it was—in the tower, banished. Your mother was a very pretty woman, but you're nothing like her physically. You're very much like your father, then again you're entirely yourself. In fact, Natalie, you're the most ravishing young creature I've ever seen, with a skin like silk!'

'The woman who loved you would have to pay and pay dearly,' she said softly.

'Keep that up, and you'll be paying yourself. Who's shaking, is it you or is it me?' Lang's hands slipped to her narrow waist and he stopped dead on the crowded floor. 'Come on, a man can take so much. Regrettably Bruce is taking you home and he's looking, at the moment, extremely anxious!'

'Anyway, I'm tired.'

'Why now? A minute ago you had stars in your eyes.'

Not so Grace. It was immediately apparent that another minute on the dance floor would have thrown her into a vicious spin. Her hand gripped at the beautiful rope of pearls that hung loosely around her neck and all her years as a civilised, sophisticated woman were made to count for nothing. Then Lang's voice rippling like black velvet suggested it was time to go home. Hours later in the dreamy little lull before she fell off to sleep Natalie touched the place on her wrist that his mouth had traced. Sensations washed all around her and she let them, too far gone now to rescue herself.

CHAPTER FIVE

In the New Year, Maccalla welcomed the British invasion in the form of Andrew Calvert's first cousin, Richard, along with his wife, Louise and their four children—Mark, Matthew, Sarah and John, their names being coincidental and not a result of their parents' passion for the Bible. It was young John with a finely tuned nervous system and a worsening, unshakeable bronchial condition who had not only made the trip advisable but pressing. Winter at home could no longer be considered and the two cousins, who corresponded frequently, decided the best and most harmonious solution would be to unite the two families under the brilliantly fine and dry Australian sun.

Their English cousins needed little enticement. Separated by more than fourteen thousand miles, they were still very close. Indeed it had been Louise with her husband's full approval and encouragement who had written to Natalie in the early days of the estrangement asking her to share their home with them. Loath though they were to interfere in this painful and seemingly inexplicable situation, for they had not met Britt, the thought of Natalie being on her own with her grandmother, Lady Sabien, now gone, troubled this English branch of the family for some years, even with Natalie a constant correspondent. She had been very much in their hearts and minds since they had first met her when she had been little older than their own Jo-Jo. In the tragic days after Nadia's death Drew Calvert had taken his daughter abroad in an effort to distract a young mind that was fretting badly. The Calvert family home in Surrey had been their base during an extended tour of Britain and the Continent. So they were none of them strangers. Richard and Louise had twice been out to Australia in the days when Nadia had been alive, so it was only a first for Sarah and Jo-Jo, who were excited 'out of their minds'.

The family coming over to them made an enormous difference to Natalie and her father, like some wonderful grace note. All of them had a great feeling of family, enchanced by compatible personalities and temperaments. Even Britt rose to the occasion, seeing it as a challenge, not being so sufficiently far gone that she couldn't resurrect her former congenial manner, laughing at all Richard's continuous sardonic little quips and sallies and scintillating herself over many an excellent dinner.

Richard's resemblance to his cousin and hence to Natalie and Natalie to her two youngest cousins was quite the subject for mention, the two older boys being the image of their mother. All the young Calverts responded miraculously to the sunny side of things, spending a good deal of their time between sightseeing excursions in Maccalla'. beautiful swimming pool with plenty of adjacent sunning and entertainment area in the angled deck. Never except for parties had the barbecue and food serving facilities been put to such use. With both of his older brothers undertaking to teach him to swim Jo-Jo was just starting to show the visible benefits of lots of sunshine and a fine, proven therapy for his condition.

Increasingly career-orientated with the project house, Natalie found Louise's presence in the house acted as a charm. Louise was a marvellously serene, very charming woman of uncanny sensitivity and the golden looks of a goddess, and she provided a wonderful balance between Natalie and her step-mother, whose sense of frustration was lifted drama-tically as new interests and new enthusiasms began to pour into the house. Friends kept popping in, attracted into the house to meet the cousins, and social pleasures and activities were plentiful. Britt simply found she didn't have the time for her usual uptight moments, and to top it all Drew declared that nothing would give him greater pleasure than to open up Maccalla's wonderful ballrooms for a party. 'No, not a party, hang it, but the never-to-be-forgotten excitement and extravagance of a real ball!'

Everyone thought it a brilliant idea, providing Drew just sat back and relaxed out of the areas of activity which could prove tiresome for him. He had already fended off any unspoken suggestions that perhaps his health was not up to a large-scale entertainment. His cousin, looking at him with affectionate, searching eyes, saw no reason why he shouldn't give a ball in his own home and enjoy it for a few hours. The womenfolk would handle everything and he was well up to checking the con-tents of the cellar.

A mood of expansive goodwill and enthusiasm swept through the house, favourably and unobtrusively stagemanaged by Louise, who had exceptional experience and a natural ability for handling people. Nothing required more attention and patience than bringing up three boys, she laughingly remarked to her husband in the luxurious privacy of Maccalla's best guest suite, so handling Britt was no real problem for a woman with many unwritten diplomas. What she did not say was that Jo-Jo had nearly worn out all her energies, and she was a woman of vigour. There had been very few moments free of anxiety with Jo-Jo's too frequently recurring bad attacks. Some drugs had proved too severe for his system and he was woefully thin with a concave little slant to his chest. Now mother and son were finding their energies glowingly replenished in the fire of the sun, a whole storehouse of vitality.

Louise had cause to be grateful to Janet Hood, Drew's nurse, who had instituted a light programme of physiotherapy for Jo-Jo which she and Uncle Drew managed to turn into a game as Drew and young Jo-Jo took their exercise together. All the loose ends so far as Louise was concerned were being taken care of, which was a blessed relief.

Natalie, too, had found a new freedom, even if she was working harder than ever before in her life. The major room of the project house, the living–dining room, was completed, and she had only to carry her single concept of planning into the other areas of the house. The entire household, which now included Janet and excluded Britt who was more importantly caught up in the social milieu had seen over the whole estate and pronounced judgment on Natalie's efforts, using little Sarah's newest word and a very old one in the Australian idiom: 'Beaut!' This her father interpreted as 'displaying tremendous imaginative power'.

Lang, from the final editing which excluded only one hand-woven tapestry and a few details of lighting, seemed to agree. Abnormally hard pressed and in fact rushed off his feet, he still found the time to accompany them around, explaining each major innovation in turn, arousing his usual gratifying, highly favourable response in people, even little people like the children, for the family so far as Natalie could see chalked up his tour as a highlight of the visit. A man of exceptional physical and mental endowments was bound to be noticed, and all of them were of the creative spirit, especially Jo-Jo, who wanted to be an architect like Uncle Drew—not surprising when his parents were culturally involved to an impressive degree. Matthew, who had inherited his mother's golden good looks, even suggested taking a final year at Timbertop. If it was good enough as a school for Prince Charles then it should get him off to a good start as well. Mark, his shadow and less articulate, thought it might be important for him too. There could be no financial problem, for Richard Calvert was managing amazingly well to keep afloat in a world awash with economic crises. Every new business venture he took on prospered, and there were important developments on this side of the world that he might find time to look into.

So for a while for Natalie the world was just a giant chandelier, each day touched with some kind of glory. She found in Louise the womanly radiance, the comfort and the companionship she had loved and then lost with her own mother's passing. These days, Maccalla seemed to be putting its house in order, but it was only the Divine hand of Providence sending through the great sun to dispel five undeserved years of living in shadow.

Andrew Calvert recognised it for what it was—a compensation. But no matter. He was moving through a country of his own and in it he was no stranger. Each day dawned like a miracle, the bold, brilliant sun spilling majestically into his room, warming his leaden limbs to life, and strangely he was happy as he had never been happy before, as if he had valiantly accepted a hard, painful lesson and reaped the reward. The sight of his daughter, so beautiful, so happy, so clearly displayed the gifts she had inherited from him, thanked him over and over again. He had Richard who understood him like his own mirror image, Louise was a woman like Nadia had been, and the child brought the house to life again, young Jo-Jo, his constant little companion, looking so much better than when he had first arrived.

Britt! ... well, Britt no longer bewildered him, no longer hurt him as she had done with whole days lapsing before she came near him and then only for a few minutes. Britt could not tolerate illness. She was a strange woman, seized by many inner struggles, full of secrets and schemes. He had never really known her. Britt was a closed book.

Perhaps if she had borne a child.... But he could no longer think about that. His daughter had been returned to him and she was blameless, of everything. When Lang called in that afternoon he would ask him to hang the big portrait again. Lang was quality, a man of integrity and wholeness, yet he didn't really know Britt either. Britt had a feline capacity for camouflaging the truth. Behind her long golden eyes there lurked a cunning of which she was proud. She had changed their very existence, shrouding Maccalla in unhappiness with a pointless, cruel victory. Natalie was his rightful heir, and the portrait was to change everything. It might have been a poisonous vine Britt saw hanging on the wall, not Natalie's silvery fair mother and a child with long black hair and a magnolia skin. After that, Britt became unreachable and the wildness that was in her was soon to find a release. Sensing this, Janet watched over her patient carefully.

Celebrations often terminate in arguments, and Maccalla's gala ball was to be no exception, but for its guests at least, the evening's entertainment was to prove brilliant. The top social strata, fiercely competitive of their parties and functions, were made to see what real style was at some level that had passed right beyond the mere possession of a great deal of money.

Andrew Calvert had achieved his ambition to see the magnificent old ballroom glitter into life again, and he was never to see it again. For most of the evening Britt, disguised as a strikingly good-looking woman in an amber silk ball gown with diamonds in her ears and at her throat, kept the violent churning of her mind well hidden, but her compulsions were driving her towards malice. The portrait, reinstated after its years in obscurity, was an intolerable insult, something Drew had dredged up to torment her. Miles Langford, the artist, had flown many hundreds of miles to be at the party and during the course of the evening he stated that the portrait was probably one of the best things he had done. That remark alone magnetised most of the guests into the library where the painting hung just left of the fireplace.

It was a portrait in the grand tradition, compounded of great technical skill and a sweeping, romantic panache. Against the dark background Nadia Calvert's ash-gold hair and fair, translucent skin shimmered like a pink-lustred pearl. Against Nadia's filmy dress and the lovely blue-patterned silk of the carved giltwood chair, Natalie emerged like some exotic elfin child, with a white matt skin quite different in texture from her mother's and her hair sweeping around her small face like black velvet. The great sapphire that glowed on her mother's hand Natalie wore tonight.

When her father first saw her he thought she couldn't possibly be as beautiful as she seemed to him that night. Then when he saw other people stopping dead in their tracks to stare at her a great feeling of wonder and love spread through him. Her beauty wasn't just physical; it had something more important, an appeal to the spirit and the intellect as well. With her shoulder-length hair, her grey eyes and her finely cut features she had an air of breeding of which everyone was aware, but Natalie herself was unaware of the effect she was creating. She was never still, going from one partner to the other, as beautifully lighthearted and sparkling as the champagne that flowed freely.

By ten o'clock the ball was in full swing and Britt had the smile frozen to her face. She felt bitterly rejected and uncared-for, as though she saw the hanging of the portrait as a major infidelity of her husband's. The large oval mirror over the white marble mantelpiece reflected the two superb chandeliers that lit the large room and the brilliant kaleidoscope of colours in the women's swirling dresses. It might have been a scene out of a past era. Down the length of the room Natalie, in her extravagantly beautiful ball gown that could have come straight out of *Gone With the Wind*, was being twirled with enthusiasm and not a good deal of expertise by Bruce Duncan, of whom Britt had never approved. He had never shown her the proper deference, and Britt's eyes narrowed dangerously.

'Britt! Can I get you some champagne?' Lang's voice cut in. He had moved from the old billiard room where all the liquid refreshments were being served, and stood a little to the side of her, watching the direction of her gaze. 'They make a handsome couple, as the saying goes!'

She turned to him as though she desperately needed the reassurance of his presence. 'Then why doesn't he take her away? She's given him enough encouragement.'

'Has she? I thought we were keeping her a little

too hard at it myself. She looks about as fragile as a piece of Chantilly porcelain, and every bit as beautiful.'

'Men are always ensnared by a pretty face!' Britt said very bitterly.

'And why not? It would be pretty dull having to stare after Bruce.'

'That girl was born to bring trouble,' Britt muttered with increasing pessimism, and her cousin glanced at her sharply.

'Get a hold of yourself, Britt!'

'I must speak to you,' she said suddenly, urgently.

'What do you suggest?' To his own surprise his voice came out very pleasantly indeed. 'We can't just duck behind those little gilt chairs. What is it, Britt? You sound distraught when you should be enjoying yourself.'

'Can you wonder!' she answered so jaggedly that he took her arm and led her over to the french doors. 'How *could* you have told her?'

'Listen, Britt,' he said with marked patience, 'I'm not with you at all. Aren't you being just a wee bit theatrical?'

'I don't think so at all. This thing you and Bart Hayes are planning—it would hurt Drew dreadfully if he knew you were making plans without him, almost as though you thought he was finished. And Natalie? What sort of a double game is she playing? You gave her this commission, yet she schemes behind your back. No doubt she wants her father to finance her in a business of her own. Too much encouragement has gone to her head, and you're very much at fault there.'

'Slow down,' he ordered, and his blue eyes flashed fire. 'This seems to be choking you, Britt, so start right at the beginning.'

'You'd scarcely want this news to get to Drew?' she challenged him. 'Why, it might kill him!'

'So far as I'm aware,' he said, and his voice warned her, 'there *is* no news.'

'According to Drew's daughter, you plan to head a conglomerate corporation and you want Drew out!'

'Natalie never said that,' snapped Lang, and he looked quite frightening with his back to the glittering shower of lights.

'And I'm lying?' Britt gave a peculiar little laugh.

'I'm not quite sure what you're doing, Britt, nor why.'

'I'm trying to help *you*, Lang. And my husband!'

'Oh? I thought you'd forgotten him of late.'

'So she's got to you too?'

'Stick to the point!' he said harshly. 'You started this.' He was so tense his eyes were flashlit, incredibly blue. 'It's difficult to find people so dangerously single-minded, Britt. If you're out to discredit Natalie, this story of yours doesn't have the right ring.'

Britt's nerves were too ragged to tolerate this shocking swing away in allegiance. Lang had been her confidant for so long, now to turn away from her in a matter of seconds, his vivid eyes contemptuous. There was a hard arrogance about him that released memories of their grandfather whom the whole family had called Black Jack to his back. She could feel the frightening wildness rise in her and she whirled on him like a tigress.

'You seem to be ignoring the dreadful possibility that she'll go to Drew with your story!'

'If any story gets to Drew,' he said curtly, 'I'll hold you responsible! And Britt, have a care! I'm not Drew, a gentleman through and through and never contradict a lady. There's more than a touch of the old Frazer ruthlessness in me, though you seem to have the lion's share. I think you were counting on the fact that I'd believe you at all costs. For some reason Natalie unloosens the destructive forces in your nature. Your jealousy is almost psychopathic, and now I'm aware of it. It makes me question all your old confidences. There was so little you left me to surmise, and I might have believed you for ever had I not met Natalie. Whatever her faults, and I can't think of one off-hand, she's not vindictive. It's as foreign to her nature as it's innate in yours. All this has been a great deal with me lately. You see, at the beginning I gave Natalie a hard time of it. I suppose I still do. I was always looking for some reason to doubt her, but that's a lack in me. I've never particularly liked women.'

'Oh, that's good!' Britt laughed rather crudely.

'If you mean I could have had my pick of a lot of women in this very room, that's not at all the same thing.'

'And I'm totally unprepared for this staggering reaction of yours,' Britt burst out, her face flushing darkly. 'I had to speak to you tonight, in your own interests.'

'Knock it off, Britt, though you play the part of a

woman wronged to perfection. Now I realise your feelings towards Natalie transcend all normal dislike. I suppose we could agree on the fact that you hate her and you'll snatch at anything to harm or discredit her. Somehow you picked up this story yourself. You have a way of finding things out and any amount of leisure time to go ferreting.'

Britt's eyes glowed and winked like a jungle cat's. Her jealousy poured out in a sickening flood. 'Go to her!' she bared her teeth, her eyes avid, 'and to hell with you both!'

'Thank you!' His blue narrowed eyes fixed very coldly on her face. 'You know, Britt, starting this kind of thing, especially now, shows a definite lack of style, and that's what they've got, the Calverts—style. Even you couldn't deny that!'

Britt seemed to crumble inside. 'It's incredible!' she said huskily. 'For you to turn on me so viciously.'

'Well, I've never particularly liked you, Britt,' he said pleasantly, 'but I never knew you carried poison inside you. None of us are free to go our own way. There have to be a few rules to abide by to avoid *self*-destruction, if nothing else.'

Britt's whole body was flicking and her amber eyes glinted quite startlingly sinister. 'You're heartless, and it's all because of that treacherous girl. When you find out the truth about this, it will be much too late. I wouldn't meet you around the corner!'

This appeared to amuse him, and his intensely masculine face was very hard and scornful. 'Forgive me, my dear, if I don't consider the loss of your friendship a disaster.'

Britt threw back her tawny head that had taken her hairdresser three hours to effect. Her long creamy throat rippled, but not a sound came out. Lang gave her a brief smile that was as dangerous as a discharge of lightning. He looked, had he known it, as formidable as the devil himself, and points of alarm started to flicker in Britt's eyes.

'It might be as well for you to reassess the situation,' he said coldly. 'If Natalie can't defend herself, and I don't suppose she's learned all that much in this jungle world of ours, *I will*!'

'I think you'll find Grace will have a few objections!' Britt said with uncontrolled malice.

'Grace?' Lang swung his imperious dark head down the room to where Grace Copeley was the centre of her own small charmed circle. She had her crisply curled head thrown back, laughing uproariously at some sally or other, absolutely stunning in a jade green satin evening gown with enormous appliqués of embroidered flowers. 'I can't see I owe Grace Copeley anything.'

'You're cruel!' said Britt as though seeing the hard planes of his face for the first time.

There was a momentary gleam in his very blue eyes. 'And it's just as well that you know. Natalie is only a babe in the wood where you and Grace are concerned, and Britt,' he cautioned her lightly, 'I'm on Natalie's side!'

Britt stood looking after him and she shivered as if an icy stream of air was playing over her face and throat. Though she shied away from it passionately, Lang had come to find her out. In spite of his open contempt she wanted to call him back, explain her position; it would be a nightmare if Lang deserted her. She watched him move very purposefully towards Natalie, the contrast between her black hair, her white skin and the crystal clarity of her eyes never more apparent. Lang carried her away from her partner with ruthless efficiency and a tantalising male grace. Britt sucked in her breath and wished that a great wind would blow up and drive them both into hell.

For the first time that night Natalie experienced a feeling of utter weightlessness, as though no one but Lang could match her lovely dancing movements. Her slender young body was full of unconscious allure and he held her close and completely acquiescent in his arms. The champagne, the music and the heady adulation she had undoubtedly received were all merging intoxicatingly together, but nothing could compare with the unfaltering excitement and magic of being in Lang's arms.

'You're not sorry, are you, Natalie, I took you from your partner?' his voice softly mocked her.

'No.' She looked up at him with her wide, black-lashed eyes. It would be hell to love Lang with no hope of return. 'I thought you were only trying to hurt me a little,' she explained. 'This is our first dance this evening.'

'But we both knew it would happen.'

'*I* wasn't sure.'

His blue eyes glittered all over her face and rested on her mouth. 'Not good enough, Natalie.'

'I really wasn't sure,' she persisted, every nerve in her body responding to his touch. Acutely sensi-

145

tive, she recognised the hidden tension in him. 'What is it?' she asked him, some strangeness in his eyes as he looked at her, disturbing. 'It can't be the old patterns repeating. You were talking to Britt.'

'Yes. She was giving me some advice.'

'I thought you considered that tabu in a woman.'

'You're right. Tell me, little one, can you see some resemblance between Britt and me?'

'No, not the slightest. Why?'

'Oh, never mind. What does it matter?'

'Britt talks a strange language I've never heard of before,' she said, giving way to a little flicker of fear.

'I can't deny that. You're a very nice little girl, Natalie, with your cloud of black hair. When are you going to allow yourself to love someone other than your father?' His blue gaze was very relentless on her face, lingering on the pulse that started to beat frantically in her throat.

'No one plans things like that!' she sighed with a touch of real melancholy.

'Falling in love? Natalie, you look so heartbreakingly beautiful we might just glide through those french doors and let the night swallow us up.'

'Have you ever loved anyone?' she dared asking him.

'That's my secret!' A kind of hard recklessness was on him and she realised he was not being flippant at all but in dead earnest.

'Yes, that's right,' he said as her slight body trembled against him. 'I want to kiss you breathless. Frightening, isn't it? What did you expect, with the sight of you burning into my memory?'

'And there's something else to it, isn't there?' she said, her voice soft, her eyes a silvery dazzle with the colour rushing up under her skin. 'Something's upset you. Something rather cruel and unpleasant.'

'I haven't the heart to get the words out tonight. What colour is it, your dress?'

'*Bleu celeste*.' She answered him automatically, her mind diverted elsewhere, but whatever *he* thought it only made him smile.

'I'm not very familiar with your smile,' she said, realising with a pang that there was some inexplicable little tension in him. 'And it's so terribly attractive. Tell me, is it true what everyone is saying tonight, and you and Grace Copeley are going to make a match of it?'

'A mess of it might be more accurate, and I mean no disrespect to Grace. It's just that Grace likes to direct and I follow a course of my own. It doesn't take much in-depth psychology to see that wouldn't work. Besides, there's some major weakness in all this. I've never said at any time of my life I was marrying anyone.'

'That's pretty extreme, isn't it?'

'Perhaps I've never known what I really wanted up until now. Now I simply want to make love to you, so if you're frightened you'd better run for your life.'

A wild impulse to tell him she loved him died in her. He would only laugh and say she didn't know what love was at all. His eyes had the same deep blue colour of the sapphire on her hand, and from bubbling exhilaration she became suddenly serious.

The passion that was upon her was of mind and of body, and she knew she didn't have the strength or the determination to fight him. It was a vital necessity to stay right there in his arms, moving with a dreamlike fascination.

'What are you thinking, it's useless to struggle?'

'I'm thinking you have some kind of black magic for me,' she admitted.

'Why *black*?' he demanded, holding her away from him, looking into her face with striking intensity. 'It seems exquisitely right to me.' His hand moved gently, touching her cheek, mocking her.

'You're hypnotising me!' she whispered.

'Why, because I want you to look at me?'

'Something has happened to me, because I can't look away.'

'The truth is, Natalie, you don't want to, and I'm equally dependent on you. That's just the way it is —unsought but inescapable!'

She became agonisingly aware of his hand on the bare skin of her back. The hand holding her tightened. 'Natalie—' There was a faint break in his voice. The french doors were open, the curtains moving, the garden heavy with the scent of the roses, like incense falling all round them. Lang picked her up as easily as if she were a child, his footsteps moving with soft thuds over the velvet pile of the grass, on to the infinite, leafy caverns of the trees.

They were alone in a silent world of the senses and he set her on her feet, keeping one arm around her swaying figure, turning her fully towards him with quickening urgency.

'I don't know if nothing makes sense, or you're the only sense there is!'

The leaves trembled and their fresh, aromatic scent shivered in the night air. The moon glittered in her eyes, shimmering silver, and lit the smooth pearl of her skin, and Lang pulled her towards him with a sweet, subdued violence that was an act of love in itself. His lips touched her throat, then her mouth, calling up a blinding response that was indescribably romantic, full of a nostalgic abandon. There was no corner of her mind she could withdraw to, nor would he have permitted it.

In his arms, she told him the untellable, the impossible—she loved him. Loved everything about him, his whole aura, but it was soundless, lost in mounting crescendoes, like an obsessive dream from which she never wanted to awaken.

'I just want to go on kissing you, never stopping!' He lifted his head as though he had no faith at all in his own sense of control and the moon fell across her face again, illuminating it intensely. 'I wanted that, Natalie, since I first laid eyes on you, the breeze sweeping your hair and whipping the silk of your dress. I knew then that I was moving into some new dimension. Either I've given up all my old ideas or my vision has become sharper. Which is it? You won't tell me!'

Natalie tried to speak, but no words would come. She was lost in some incomprehensible world where she was owned body and soul. Lang's hand shaped her face and she thought, you won't say you *love* me. Perhaps you never will, yet it seems to me I've always known and loved you, unreservedly. Such an infinite difference between us! Yet when he caught her intriguing, love-lost, loving, soft young face again, she didn't resist him but gave herself up completely because that was the way he had with her. Pride was of little consequence when his hard, caressing mouth was turning her heart over and over again. A thin stratum of her mind recognised it would have to stop, but she was powerless to stop anything.

His mouth left hers so abruptly she could have cried out with the pain of loss, yet his hands as he shook her were exquisitely gentle.

'Natalie, alias camellia-face, you throw me completely off balance. Either we go back to the house or we run away!' he said ardently.

'Where?'

'Oh, somewhere I'll never let you out of my sight again!' He stood arrested, one hand uplifted to fold back her black sweep of hair, when a woman's shockingly clear voice rent the air:

'What's all this cloak and dagger stuff?' Grace Copeley was moving very swiftly indeed towards them, unmistakable bitter sarcasm in her tones.

'Nothing like that at all, Gracie,' Lang responded urbanely. 'I don't give a damn if the whole world sees us!'

'Now that does give me pause!' She jerked up a hand to her throat. 'You realise, of course, my dear, Lang excels at all these rendezvous under the stars.'

'You must recall, Gracie, we've never had one!'

'Oh, please!' Natalie could feel the other woman's pain and embarrassment. 'It's simply that I wanted a breath of fresh air!'

'Instead of which you appear to have plunged into a first-class love affair!'

'Take it or leave it, Gracie,' said Lang, his head thrown back, very emphatically, arrogantly male.

'You're a cruel devil, Lang!' Grace Copeley burst out, with extreme desolation, as if she was about to burst into sobs.

'Please, I'm going!' Natalie protested, swamped by the thought of such a spectacle.

'Then you'll damn well go by yourself,' Grace reverted to her usual sharp vigour. 'Lang, I want you to stay right here.'

'Do you wonder, Gracie, your marriage broke up!' he said suavely. 'Men just don't like all these immoderate demands.'

'She's not the one for you!' said Grace, wild and sudden, and obviously in a bad way. 'Why, she's little more than a child and you go overboard for her! Oh yes, she's clever! I've been over the house with Bart Hayes....'

'Stop there!' he ordered, and there was danger all around him. 'Britt too?'

'Britt?' she said vaguely as though he had introduced some pointless line of thought. 'Yes, of course, Britt, as it happens. Britt arranged the whole thing. I mean, she's known Nancy Hayes for years. What is this, anyway?'

'What was it you talked about?' he persisted, vaguely suggesting that he was lining up some fairly serious indictments.

'Nothing. Absolutely nothing. I mean, I couldn't break right out and say it was sensational, which it is, it wouldn't have earned me any high grades with

Britt. She loathes this girl, didn't you know?'

'As a matter of fact, I did!'

'Well, I don't mind telling you, you two-fisted devil, no good will come of it. I can't imagine how you thought it would!'

'Destiny!' said Lang, sounding harshly amused. 'Destiny's direction. What good is a career to me without the most beautiful woman in the whole of Adelaide?'

'Darling!' Grace looked hopeful and heart-broken at once.

'While you debate this thing out, I'm going back to the house,' Natalie said shakily, starting to feel the first waves of implication. What *was* all this about Britt, Bart Hayes, the project house? She had the notion Grace Copeley didn't know, but Lang did. The thought made her anxious and uneasy. Britt always took good care to run her right into a corner—an indefensible position.

'Gracie and I haven't a thing to talk about!' said Lang, his hand closing on her arm, quick and hard.

'Actually a great deal!' snapped Grace. 'Let the child go.'

'No!'

That emphatic decision was not lost on either of them. Grace's significant glance sped through the air like a poisoned dart. 'Quite frankly,' she said kindly, 'I think you're making a big mistake, Lang, but I see now you're a man who needs plenty of rope.'

'My dear,' he said cuttingly, 'don't confuse me with your husband. No good could come of it.'

'I don't envy you the brute!' Grace said painfully to Natalie. 'Any woman who gets tangled up with Lang Frazer is just begging for regrets!'

'Well, those I'm not looking for,' Natalie said quietly. 'I'm sorry, Miss Copeley, I wouldn't hurt you for the world!'

'And I don't suppose you would!' Grace said oddly. 'I haven't been so generous to another woman for very many years.'

'At this rate, we'll all finish up friends again!' Lang looked at both of them approvingly, diabolically male and too sure of himself.

'No!' Natalie's cry sounded like a wounded bird's. 'I'm not going to be taken over by anyone!' She broke Lang's firm hold and gathered up her dress with swift impulsiveness, feeling the dark rush of mutiny.

Lang's voice throbbed with a kind of cool passion that utterly shook her.

'Natalie!'

But she only wanted to get away, fluttering fears winging all around her, a lightning transition from trembling submission to a desire to assert her own personality, throw off the trancelike excitement.

Grace's voice reached her with a brittle little laugh in it. 'Now that girl is showing sense!'

'Shut up, Gracie,' said Lang Frazer, unforgivably insolent, but Grace only smiled. For all her sophistication she couldn't hide her feeling for this man. He was a convulsive, dangerous excitement and she would punish herself over and over again just for a few hours of his company. After tonight she would be haunted by the way he held the girl, Natalie, in

153

his arms. He had never, never kissed her like that, but she had the pathetic longing that he might.

Finally Lang took her arm, his mood brutal, leading Grace back over the grass towards the brilliantly lit house. 'Young girls are all rabbits!' Grace said helpfully.

'Let's have a drink!'

'It helps a good deal!' Grace brightened like a sunflower, warmed by the touch of his hand on her bare arm, sparking off heaven knew how many wanton little thoughts, thinking not deeply, but somewhat that the status quo had been restored. A clever, mature woman was worth any dozen green girls.

Long after they had all gone home, leaving not one case of champagne unopened, Britt did her usual over-stimulated circuit of her room. The whole brilliant evening was flawed for her, her whole way of life threatened. No use to look for pity or compassion from Lang either. He had gone over to the enemy—unthinkable, but there it was, a very bitter pill. She had never known such a terrible sense of aloneness. From now on it would be fight all the way. She paused at her bedside table and took a cigarette from the ivory box on it. She lit it, drew in, coughed and started to laugh, all in a few hysterical eruptions. As she laughed she drew still more smoke into her lungs, and the door adjoining her and her husband's suite of rooms opened and Andrew came rather haltingly in.

'What is it, Britt? I couldn't help hearing.'

'Nothing. A drink of water. *Please*,' she added,

her nostrils flaring, her face wild and wary.

He looked at her closely and went through to the luxurious white and gold mirrored bathroom and found a glass, filling it quickly with water. When he came back Britt had regained her breath and partial control of herself. She was sunken now in a silk damask armchair, looking very white now the coughing fit had passed, without make-up, older, sadder, even tragic. She accepted the glass from his hand, sipped at it as if its contents could very well contain strychnine, then she passed the glass back to him with a grimace so he could put it down again.

'You didn't enjoy yourself tonight, did you?' he asked, moving back and lowering himself very slowly on the bed they had once shared.

'And that's the difference between us,' she said in a deadly sort of tone. 'You seemed to be having a wonderful time, though you look very tired now.'

Andrew Calvert was determined to avoid all catastrophes. 'What happened to us, Britt?' he asked in a gentle, very humble tone that strangely enough she deplored.

She shrugged and shifted her position rather frantically. 'You can't mean to start up an enquiry now,' she said tightly. 'I mean, these things happen, Drew.'

His expensive dark red silk dressing gown hung on his thin frame, belted very tightly around his narrow waist, but incongruously his lean narrow feet were thrust into his very oldest, most comfortable slippers. Drew, who was always immaculately fastidious. There was a terrible frailty about him all of a sudden and Britt felt the full weight of it.

'Just after your stroke,' she said unhappily, passing a weary hand over her face, 'when you were in intensive care, I thought I'd go out of my mind with worry and despair. I did love you, Drew.'

'But not now. Not the way I am,' he said abruptly.

'Everyone seems to think you'll get entirely well again!'

'Everyone but you and me!'

Her head spun around and she could only stare at him. 'What do you mean?'

'Don't look so startled, Britt. I've come damn near to dying, and that says a lot.' His grey eyes were contemplative. 'Tell me, was it true about our child? All these years and I've never really known.'

Britt dropped her gaze and began to swing her long perfect legs back and forth. 'Of course it was!' she said violently, and just the way she said it dispelled his very last illusion.

A look of agonised concentration came into his face. 'Perhaps everything would have been all right for us, without Natalie, my little girl. Without wanting it, or understanding it, she acted as a catalyst!'

'I'm quite sure of it!' Britt said heavily. 'This house, for instance, would be mine. As it is, I'm never quite sure of it.'

'Is that what you married me for, the house?' he asked her with no trace of censure.

'I told you,' she said turbulently, 'I loved you— your looks and your brilliance and your lifestyle.

And this wonderful house! It impels me to do certain things.' Her face twisted in pain or an agony of shame as if she realised her behaviour was shoddy in such infinite elegance. 'Sometimes I wish we could start all over again, somewhere else where I might have been different.'

'If you can accept that, Britt, then there's a chance for you. Why don't you seek a little help? Speak to someone professional about all these worries that are pressing you down.'

'The city is full of psychiatrists, if that's what you mean?'

'Pick the right man and he might be able to help you, and I think you know, Britt, you need help!'

'Well, really, Drew, I'm sorry if you're brooding about all this, but I need no one. Why don't you go? You've already said too much!'

'Keep yourself in check, Britt,' he said quietly. 'This is still my house. Everything in it belongs to me—including you.'

She saw how serious he was and she looked shakily into space; her sense of being on her own was overwhelming. 'You're all against me, even Lang!'

'Why Lang, and why now?' he enquired. 'Because his eyes follow Natalie wherever she goes?'

'You don't miss a thing, do you?' she muttered, her eyes on the carpet, but he continued to observe her thoughtfully.

'My heart goes out to you, Britt, the way you punish yourself. On the other hand I cannot allow you to keep punishing the rest of us. Lang is still your friend.'

'He's not in the least,' she moaned in a helpless

fit of rejection. 'Don't boost me up. Myself, I don't think much of traitors!'

Andrew pulled away from her almost visibly as if she was a black spider. 'What can that mean?'

'Nothing. Forget it,' she threw out with considerable asperity. 'You look worn out, Drew. Go to bed.'

'Pardon me, my dear, but I'll make my own mind up. It's very clear of late. Besides, I want to make my peace with you, but you won't let me.'

She looked over at him with astonishment, as though his suggestion was as unexpected as it was unwelcome. 'I'm overcome, Drew, and let's leave it there. Lang, by the way, has some plan for starting out on his own!' Her voice was full of a hateful antagonism and Drew Calvert knew it for what it was—a deliberate piece of dishonesty. It was just like Britt to drive on. He shook his head emphatically, but the blood rushed to his brain and his heart started up a slow laboured thudding.

'Now that, my dear, I won't have. Instinct and experience tell me it's simply not true.'

'All right, don't believe me,' she said. 'It's no skin off my nose. According to Nance Hayes, however, Lang is spending a lot of time dreaming up heading a big conglomerate corporation.'

'Britt, my dear,' he said a little wearily, 'you're in your domain again, making trouble. It's belittling and it will cripple your spirit. Lang did mention some such thing to me once, about a year ago, and then only in passing. We were too busy then to go into it, but Lang being Lang I knew he would bring it up again. Lang is much more of a business man than I am, but he's happy working with me as I am with him. We have the most prestigious firm in the city.'

Britt avoided his glance and wrapped her arms about herself as if she was freezing. 'Lang is ambitious as you've never been!'

'That's true!' he observed calmly, 'but Lang is a man of integrity. I know it and you know it, so why on earth should you insist on trying to deceive me? The truth will out, Britt, no matter how long it takes, and God knows there has to be a time to repent. You can't touch me any more, so it must be Natalie. It's always been Natalie. Have you concocted yet another story about her?'

'No story. Harsh fact,' Britt said with incurable venom and a near-pathological belief in herself. 'Lang didn't believe me either, but he will.'

A look of the greatest relief crossed Drew Calvert's face. He looked almost radiant. 'Good for Lang! I didn't realise how much he knew. Why, you're nothing but a coward, Britt, and don't cowards like to hand out the punishment! Lang, I think, loves my daughter, and that makes me very happy and content.'

Britt thrust her head forward, rage in her heart. She had gone beyond all point of reclamation, when she became insensible to what she was doing, upsetting a man more gravely ill than she knew.

'It's time I took matters into my own hands,' she said, with a flash of sheer callousness. 'Natalie and Lang just will not do. I'll never allow it!'

Into her husband's face came an expression of pained contempt mingled with pity. 'Think on this, Britt. We all have to reap what we sow, and for you the harvest could be bitter indeed. It's for your own sake I'm saying this. I dare not be lenient with you as I have been in the past. I doubt if I have the strength to endure watching you destroy yourself. I mean this, Britt. See someone, make a confession. Janet would know a good man.'

'Janet, that woman?' she said scornfully.

'You despise all the wrong people, Britt, that's your big problem.' He got up from the bed, looking carefully around the room as though he had no real anticipation of seeing it again. Then he walked past his wife, stopping to touch her arm.

'Good night, my dear. Try to get some sleep!'

Suddenly the sight of him, the quiet cultured calibre of his voice, the enormous change that had been wrought in him, made her realise what she was doing. 'Do you hate me, too, Andrew?'

'My dear,' he said, looking full into her face. 'I've nothing but pity in my heart for you. I must confess you've always been a mystery to me and I suppose it's only fitting you should remain so. Now if you'll excuse me I'll find my own bed. You're right, you know, Britt—I'm a poor thing compared to what I was!' There was a dreadful finality in the way he spoke, as if he had become used to ticking off all the days of his life.

Britt's cheeks flamed with shame and she was overcome by great tremors of real contrition. The tears welled into her eyes and streaked across her face. She rushed to her feet and swept over to him, taking his hand and lifting it to her mouth, a rare gesture. 'Forgive me, Andrew, for everything!'

Ever after, Britt was to remember, he returned

her embrace with a smile in his fine eyes, his manner very gentle and courteous, then he turned and walked stiffly out of her life.

When Louise found him next day in his favourite seat by the lake, with the swans gliding serenely over the dark green, mirror-like surface, she could hardly believe he had gone. His face, fallen sideways, had the same sweet innocence of Jo-Jo's. Then she sank to her knees beside him, stroking his head:

'My dear, my dear!' Then, heartbroken, she burst into tears.

CHAPTER SIX

For Natalie there followed a long period of falling darkness. It was simply not possible that her father had gone. She could not come to terms with it, though Richard and Louise saw it as foreordained: their presence on Maccalla and the way they were able to lessen their young, unbearably distressed cousin's inevitable load and pain. As the weeks passed, Richard and the two eldest boys had, of necessity, to return to England, but it had been decided that Louise and the two youngest children should remain on Maccalla for an indefinite period. It was unthinkable to leave Natalie on her own and she was in no frame of mind, nor indeed fit, for travelling.

These days she cared for nothing. The roof of the world could cave in. The days passed in a haze of comings and goings and night-time, and sleep was greatly to be coveted when she could lose herself in unconsciousness. Her whole world was greyed over, without colour and sound, every word reaching her through some impenetrable fog. Then gradually for increasingly longer and longer periods, the worst pain subsided and inside she went very quiet and numb. She had loved Maccalla, her home, with a great passion. Now she felt nothing. It was just another very beautiful house that had belonged to another period of her life. The long-ago years.

Yesterday.

Louise pointed out as gently and kindly as she could that life had to go on, but for Natalie it was no more than a sad merry-go-round, for inside she was absolutely empty, floating around in some curious void. Louise saw and understood her bewilderment and pain and took over the management of the house, which Natalie very gratefully let her, but Louise had to agree with Lang when he said Natalie was like some princess in a fairytale locked away in a tower, a captive of her own quiet desperation as if she had a desire to languish away. And she wasn't going to do that! he continued, his blue eyes blazing.

Lang, Natalie avoided like the plague, and everyone knew it. Lang was cruel, overwhelming, with his probing, too intelligent eyes. It was too tiring to struggle, too tiring to be for ever on guard. It was Lang who had come to tell her of her father's death. It was into his arms she had later collapsed, but strangely, between Lang and Natalie now, there had sprung up some weird kind of throwback to the estrangement Natalie had known with her father. She had nothing whatever to say to Lang. He had to be eliminated from her world, and she could be as ruthless as he was. He could wound and rouse her, make her capable of great feeling. He made too many demands with his hard, unyielding core that demanded her total attention. Was it any wonder that she did everything possible to avoid him, exhausted and fragile, thinking up any number of excuses and manoeuvres, made all the more difficult because Louise had accepted him completely into her world, in the absence of her husband, turning to Lang with a hundred and one small matters that needed attention and advice. Then too, there was the business, and Lang had been appointed trustee for Andrew Calvert's estate. Lang didn't approve of her—Natalie knew that—nor of the way she was behaving. He would like to shake her. She could see it in his eyes as blinding blue as the sun at noon —oddly, the only colour that was seeping into her.

Lang, my love! So dreary to admit it, but Natalie never wanted to love again. Bruce was different, her friend. Gentle, undemanding, uncomplicated. Bruce wanted to help her and he told her over and over again. It was only to be expected that she should turn into Bruce's soothing, outstretched arms until life became bearable again. The children ... her own little cousins, wonderfully resilient like all children, playing happily around the beautiful grounds, inviting all their new friends in, thriving in their sun-filled environment, Jo-Jo responding miraculously to the dry heat and the daily pounding up the pool. It was occasionally in these moments, with the children hugging and kissing her, their grey eyes so like her own, very steady and gentle, that Natalie came back to anything like full awareness of life.

It was simply enough to know Louise was there in the house, but they had very little conversation. Natalie couldn't think of anything to say. Her father was dead. Maccalla was hers and she didn't want it at all. Often Louise set her a task and Natalie pretended to go to it and she did at some stage, but most of the time, she just looked into space or swam with the children in the aquamarine pool coaching little Jo-Jo who had a way of speaking about Uncle Drew every day. Very freely and naturally as his great friend who had 'gone off to Heaven', where he was as perfectly happy and safe as Jo-Jo and Sarah were at Maccalla. As simple as that. Natalie tried to see it that way, but she couldn't.

At least they were all spared Britt. Britt, now a rich woman, but deprived of all she really wanted, the property known as Maccalla, spared the agonies of grief and remorse and bolstered by the feeling she had of public outrage and humiliation, had taken herself off on an ill-deserved tour of the world, on the principle that the whole universe couldn't possibly be against her. No one was sorry to see her go. No one saw her off, but everyone was of the opinion that she would undoubtedly come back with another husband—which, in fact, she did. None of them, however, would have to be bothered with her again.

Then one day Natalie began to forget a little and allowed Bruce to take her to a friend's place for a Sunday At-Home. It was to be an informal sort of day, the sort of thing the Nicholsons did so well, with swimming, tennis, plenty of bright conversation, the most superb food, usually a barbecue in the grounds, any amount to drink and a guaranteed good time for all in lovely, semi-bushland surroundings with a stream at the back of the house, which Bruce had designed.

It was quite a drive out, but Bruce assured Natalie it would be all worth while. The Nicholsons, Stephen and Marisa, were very good value, charming and successful, and Stephen always had an extraordinary number of amusing anecdotes on call. So Natalie was content to sit quietly and let Bruce do all the thinking and deciding. She felt quite at ease with him as she did with Louise and the children, but he deserved better than this from a female companion, she thought. She didn't know the sight of her was more than enough for Bruce, the curve of her cheek, the gleaming slide of her hair, the way she folded her hands like a good little girl in her lap. She looked absolutely exquisite and unapproachable.

La Princesse Lointaine! Lang called her that. Lang was in a strange mood lately, but Bruce dared not comment on this to Natalie. They all knew the situation between Lang and Natalie and it was as puzzling as it was hard on Lang, who undoubtedly had her best interests at heart and worked very hard putting all Andrew Calvert's affairs in order. Somebody ought to talk Natalie out of it, Bruce thought, but definitely not today. It was highly unlikely that she would respond—then again, she might melt away like snow, so ethereal did she seem. Today she looked a dream in a long silky patio dress in a delicious shade of green that left her arms and her back bare and came primly to the neck, as enchanting to Bruce's mind as it was very softly sexy. But he couldn't think of that, neither that she dazzled him.

Everything in slow motion was the order of the day. Then when they arrived and Natalie got out of the car like a sinuous small cat Bruce almost groaned. There couldn't be any doubt about it, he was in love with her, but he wasn't such a fool as to think his feelings could be returned even after a fairly extensive acquaintance. Quite early, however, he had decided, in the absence of any active discouragement, that he was not going to give up. The fact that she now owned Maccalla was more a drawback than an asset so far as Bruce was concerned. He had no objection to a girl with a dowry, but Maccalla was carrying it all a bit far. A house like that would take some getting used to, but he didn't presume to think he would, one day, be asked to share it. He was supposed to find his own way in the world, but lurking beneath it all was the quite lunatic idea that Natalie might one day turn to him and say:

'I love you, Bruce!'

The very thought illuminated many a day for him even with Lang uncommonly short-tempered and working the very devil out of him. Bruce had to admit that Lang could be tough, but he was so fantastically brilliant Bruce would have jumped off a roof if Lang had asked him to as some kind of experiment. Lang's approval was of very great importance and Bruce always got a great spurt of pleasure when Lang indicated, however briefly, that Bruce was doing more than his share. All Bruce had to do now, he reasoned, was stick around and hope, though it was fairly difficult trying to court a girl who kept withdrawing all the time.

It was a glorious day in late autumn when all summer's colour and bountiful harvest had merged into red, burnished copper and gold. The sky was turquoise with the warm sun sparkling through the shuttered tops of the great gums, alive with the bittersweet warbling of birds. The deeply green grass was splashed with bright dresses in flower colours and there was a great deal of frivolity at the poolside, with one smooth-skinned redhead in a black and white bikini making something spectacular of a pretty ordinary dive. Everyone was talking, laughing, a few actively arguing, others teasing, all standing around with brimming glasses of beer or something that bubbled. A great, big, beautiful, noisy Sunday.

Stephen and Marisa were holding court under the most entrancing silver birch turned gold and Natalie was promptly taken across and taken up. Everyone suddenly knew in a chain reaction that she was Drew Calvert's daughter and they were all very kind indeed to her, recognising an expensive, patrician and very dangerous fragility about her. Bruce brought over to her a magnificent T-bone steak with various accompaniments which he later had to eat himself and they sat down at a long table in the shade of the trees looking back over the house, skirted by pines and tall eucalypts.

The house, Natalie now could see, was built on three levels, which wasn't apparent from the street entrance. It followed the slope of the land and related beautifully to its site—the stream and the native gums and the lush ferns and exotics. She fancied she could detect Lang's influence in the design and the use of the deep skylights, but she made no comment on this, merely congratulating Bruce on a fine job. It was all very distracting, the sound of music piped from the house ... Cleo Laine ... and a moving kaleidoscope of colour against the green of the trees and the grass.

Then suddenly, in their centre, whipping up instant, enormous interest, was Lang, head thrown back, calling a greeting, one hand coming up to shade his eyes from the brilliant dazzle of sun and the glare off the pool, his hand-stitched camel-coloured jacket swinging back to reveal a beautiful dark brown shirt diagonally overchecked with blue and white, casual, effortless, elegance, built into the man himself. A girl with long honey-coloured hair and carrying a guitar clung to his side like a double, her pretty face entirely serious, dedicated, a full fringe falling over her high forehead over wide, sherry-toned eyes.

For some reason Natalie chose that precise moment to ask Bruce to show her the interior of the house, shivering slightly beside him in the sparkling sunlight, like some early flowering magnolia that was about to fold its petals and not wait for spring. Somehow, despite his better judgment, Bruce found himself walking her back across the grass with Lang's wickedly mocking eyes marking their progress. Lang was *verboten* and Bruce didn't know quite what to do until Marisa saved the situation by running up, holding Lang's hand tightly and pulling him off to her own group.

Inside the large, window-walled living room, Natalie's gaze veered towards a bold graphic that dominated an end wall. It was one of Lang's, but Bruce dared not volunteer this vital piece of information. He didn't have to, as it happened, for

Natalie turned her smooth head away.

'One of Lang's?'

'Darling girl!' cried Bruce, honestly admiring. 'You're extraordinarily perceptive and so forth!'

'It looks like Lang,' she said soberly. 'He can't be anyone else but himself.'

'Now what is that supposed to mean, sweet? I think it's very good myself, and God knows he takes about two minutes to do them. Terribly effective above all those odd little sculptures, don't you think? In fact, it makes something of them. Marisa took a crash course in ceramics, otherwise she's very sweet!'

Natalie turned her satiny back very pointedly on the graphic and Bruce after a moment's hesitation charged in where angels feared to tread. 'Natalie dear, forgive my saying this, but don't you think you're making things unnecessarily complicated? With Lang, I mean. I had no idea he would be here today. He didn't say anything about it, although he has the entrée everywhere. But now that he *is* here, we can't very well avoid him. I shouldn't like to have to spend my winter in Siberia!'

'Is there any suspicion you might?' Natalie asked with a touch of Lang's own dryness.

'Well, dear ... from time to time Lang does drop a good word for me in the right places. He has a lot of influence and in a lot of diverse places.'

'That must be very helpful!' she said blandly.

'Oh, don't sound like that, baby! He's always been super to me. A trifle hellish of late, but I can stand it. Lang's heart is in the right place, believe me!'

But Natalie wasn't listening; she moved about the spacious and very original room like a blind girl. 'I think I'd like to go,' she said in a small, careful voice.

'But we've only been here a few hours!' Bruce protested. 'But yes, if you want to.'

'I'm being very selfish, aren't I?'

'Yes.' Vainly Bruce tried to jolly her out of this dangerous mood of hers, but her smoky grey eyes dilated, the pupils preternaturally large, and her gaze went beyond him.

Very thoroughly rattled, Bruce swung his head, then said, 'Oh!' in a pleased voice, his ready grin flashing. 'What brings you out here, Lang?'

'Hadn't you suspected?' asked Lang, very dryly polite. 'I came to see if you were all right, Natalie. I never get to see you these days. Like the Sleeping Beauty locked up in a glass case!'

'Oh!' said Bruce again, fascinated by this observation in depth. A tongue on him, had Lang, and diplomatically Bruce fell back a pace or two, not anxious to hamper him. He found his work much too interesting to set up any obstruction in Lang's way and he was obviously set on a course of speaking to Natalie.

'An overwhelming welcome, little one!' Lang was saying, 'though mind you, I didn't expect much else!'

There was a little pause of foreboding and Bruce judged it a good idea to disappear for a while. Natalie looked very small and fragile, but it was safe to conclude that she would be perfectly all right with Lang for ten minutes or so.

'Thirsty work these Sundays!' he said brightly, 'but it's a lovely party. I think I'll go snatch myself a drink!'

Natalie sprang to life again, as beautiful as a painting. 'No!'

'I'll be back, dear!' he said, delighted. 'Never fear!'

Lang's face was friendly but mocking. 'That depends!' he said, and Bruce couldn't fail to hear the note in his voice.

When he had gone Lang turned about to confront Natalie. 'Don't you think you might tell me what I've done? Or haven't done. Or do we have to start all over again?'

'Oh, please, Lang,' she begged, and her face was very pale above the tender green of her dress.

'Do you know you're making both of us utterly miserable?'

'Not *you*, Lang!' she said bitterly, most peculiarly near tears.

'Why not me? What's so different about me?' he challenged her, his blue eyes stripping away layer after layer of her sensitive skin.

'Everything!' Warning bells seemed to be hammering through her head, and she put her hand to her temples and turned her face away. 'I have a headache. I want to go home. Could you please tell Bruce for me?'

'Certainly!' he agreed suavely, 'if that's what you want. Aren't you going to say goodbye to Stephen and Marisa?'

'Of course,' she said, too far gone to be suspicious

of his ready compliance. 'If you'd please find Bruce for me.'

'I consider it my duty!' he said in his fathomless way. Five minutes later he was walking back across the grass to her and she stopped, distracted, looking up at him with overwhelmingly frightened eyes.

'Where's Bruce?'

'Bruce, my lamb,' he said tersely, 'is not coming. Very loyal is Bruce, a straightforward, eye-to-the-future kind of lad. I've trained him like that!'

'He's not coming!' she repeated, as though she couldn't understand it.

'Wake up from that beauty sleep!' he said with soft violence.

'You don't know how unhappy you're making me!'

'But why, Natalie? Can you tell me that?'

'I don't want to go with you,' she said rather desperately. 'We're too different.'

'You did ask me to speak to Bruce,' he said abruptly, in a take-it-or-leave-it voice. 'Well, I did, and now you have to take the consequences.'

'I shall scream. I shall faint.'

'Natalie,' he said quietly, 'I don't know how I prevent myself from just spiriting you off.'

'That's what you *are* doing, isn't it?' she asked passionately.

'I'll take you home or wherever you like.'

'Don't confuse me!' she said raggedly. She could hardly bear the sight of him and her emotions, so long restrained, were flaring into dangerous life. Her eyes swam with tears and the mad desire to run away and be caught at the same time.

'Natalie!' his tone was perfectly hard, far removed from loving. 'You're driving me quite mad. I'm asking you to come with me, and if you resist me now with so many avid glances about I swear I'll just pick you up and hurl you into the car.'

'You would! Oh, you would!' she said, aching with frustrations, then she made a bold bid to outwit him and he caught her wrist in a firm intolerable grip, a flicker of white-hot temper on his face.

It controlled her instantly, and panting and bewildered, she allowed herself to be put into his car. There was no threat he would not dare to carry out.

'Not as tender-hearted as Bruce!' he said, and his white teeth snapped.

'Don't touch me!' she said, her voice low and impassioned.

'And that, for very much longer, will be beyond my power. I won't let you go!'

She let out a long shuddering breath and he glanced at her with a blue flame in his eyes. 'You want someone to love, Natalie. Someone to love you, make love to you. I know you!'

'No!' she said fiercely.

He reversed very swiftly in the old expert way, leaving the house and returning to the city by an alternative route, or so she thought. The breeze through the window, subtly scented, was cooling her flushed skin.

'Come with me to Magda's place.'

'No!' she said, shocked. 'I couldn't bear to listen to music.'

'What are you frightened of?' His dark profile was implacable, outlined in gold.

'What is this all about, Lang? Tell me.'

'I thought I had!' he said calmly.

The powerful car was picking up speed almost imperceptibly, the landscape flashing by in a whir of green. 'You're driving much too fast!' she said half fearfully, her slender body taut.

'I didn't think you'd notice!'

'Well, I have!' she cried, and her voice broke. 'What do you want to do, kill us?'

'You silly child!' he said tenderly. 'We could just finish in jail for the night. Providing it's the same cell, I wouldn't mind!'

Sensations were coming strongly now and the blood began to beat brightly in her veins, as though from a long thaw. 'Please take me home, Lang!'

'No!' His glittering eyes stayed her.

'I wish you wouldn't stare at me like that,' she said in a husky, melancholy voice.

'Was I staring? I'm sorry. They tell me it has something to do with having blue eyes. Magda lives out on this road. You've never seen the house.'

'I won't come!' she said, which was perfectly ridiculous in a speeding car, and she heard his low laugh. 'I told you, Lang,' she began to plead with him. 'I couldn't bear to hear her play. The music!' Her small teeth closed on her bottom lip and she fell silent.

'And you're very susceptible to music, aren't you? All right, then, if it would upset you to hear her play, then just see the house. I told Magda we'd call in.'

'You couldn't have told her you would bring me?' she demanded incredulously.

'As a matter of fact, I did!'

'How could you decide such a thing?' She made a helpless little movement of her hand and he suddenly caught it and held it fast.

'Quite easily, as it happened!'

'You're a very arrogant man, Lang!'

'Tell me something I don't know!' he said a shade curtly so that she was fully aware of his lean daunting strength. 'Tell me why you've been flitting around with all the ingenuity of a butterfly avoiding me. It's been pretty hard to take, in fact, all my efforts have been gathered into this one afternoon!'

'I hope you're not trying to suggest I've been bothering you!' she asked gently. 'That sounds wonderful!'

'Wonderful to have no manners, Natalie?' he chided her. 'I mean I've been worrying about your lack of them. I have this fantasy that you'll never speak to me again, or you'll finish up like some entirely credible little girl in a book, rigid with repressions!'

To her astonishment, she laughed, a silvery cascade of sound and one he had almost forgotten. He studied her critically, noticing everything about her, his mind very clear in its purpose. A little cat's paw of wind was ruffling her hair and she had her head tilted at an angle to keep the silky, flying strands out of eyes that were shimmering like diamond chips.

'Shall I put the window up?'

'No, I like the breeze!' She ran her palely frosted fingertips over her forehead. 'My reasons for avoiding you, Lang, for what they are worth to you—your personality is too potent. Too potent for me anyway. Being with you is like going down for the third time, the ultimate in drowning. You're not like anyone else!'

'I hope not!' he said so sharply it cut her to the quick, forgetting as she did that she had flicked a raw nerve in him. Then his voice lost its tension. 'It doesn't sound much fun anyway, being like someone else. Having a double could easily trip me up. How's the headache, by the way?' he enquired, disbelievingly polite, his glance brushing her face and throat, making her more vulnerable by the minute.

'It's passing off, thank you!' she said like a small girl, and stared very resolutely out the window.

He smiled and the quirk of amusement remained in his voice. 'The party, perhaps?' he suggested. 'You're out of the way of them. If it weren't for my mad obsession with you, I would have had a very quiet day myself, but I happened to be speaking to Louise....'

'... and Louise just happened to mention that Bruce and I were going out to the Nicholsons'?'

'A masterly deduction, Natalie.'

'You and Louise have fallen into a very easy friendship, haven't you?' she asked, raptly watching his lean, clever hands on the wheel.

'I'd like to think so,' he said in response. 'Louise is an extraordinarily attractive human being. They all are, your cousins. I'd like to see them remain here. In fact I'd go a step further and say there would be no great difficulty transplanting the lot of them. I've never seen such a transformation in a child as young Jo-Jo. He must have put on five or six pounds!'

Natalie's face lit up with affection. 'The complete change in climate, I suppose, and being able to get so much swimming in. Maccalla has been wonderful for him. I've thought rather often, of late, that I might be able to lease or sell the property to them. Before Father died Richard was full of the big business developments out here!'

His shock of surprise was so genuine, his foot lifted involuntarily off the accelerator and the car slowed down like magic. 'You sell Maccalla? I can't believe it! Please say that again!'

'I'm not usually so indiscreet,' she said rather wryly, 'but it's a first to shock you, Lang. I thought it was no secret; I've changed. Maccalla has too many memories for me—happiness and sorrow. I simply can't bear to remain in it any more.'

'Oh, for God's sake give yourself a little time, Natalie. Twelve more months will make all the difference!'

If she had surprised him, he was surprising her. 'Strange that you should be counselling caution, Lang. I had the oddest impression that might please you.'

His glance whipped over her like blue lightning. 'You're damned lucky you're a girl! You need a hard slap, and if you persist, you might get one. The thing is, Natalie, I've well and truly discarded any plan that might make you unhappy. As for your own idea, I don't know. Certainly Louise and the children are happy here, mainly because of young

Jo-Jo. He's been a great cause of anxiety for Louise, she told me. As for Richard and the older boys, it might be harder to uproot them. I'm quite sure they have a very beautiful home of their own.'

'Which they could lease!' she suggested quite seriously, seeing herself in her cousins' place. 'Richard knows everyone. I'm sure he'd come up with something, and there's no one other than Richard and Louise I would want to have it. In any case, it's just an idea I pulled out of the air. Oh, not quite that. I can tell Louise has come to love Maccalla and old Sir Richard is the living spit of Jo-Jo. We've all laughed about that. The thing is, Lang,' and her voice suddenly broke, 'I want to go away, all by myself!'

'You silly little goose! Why, that's perfect. *All by yourself*. You fascinate me, Natalie, you really do. You're an enigma of the first rank. Either that or you're tied up in knots. One way or the other, I'm going to find out!'

It sounded a distinct warning, very tersely dynamic, and she swung her head towards him, her eyes widening at such a brutal attack. There was a sensual ironic twist to his mouth and a quiver of fright shook her. 'With everyone else trying to be kind to me, Lang, you haven't forgotten how to thrash me verbally!'

'My love, I wouldn't hurt a hair of your head. I've come to learn patience—I've had to. You see, Natalie, I've settled on you with a very cool fanaticism. Blame it on yourself. You shouldn't have set out to seduce me!'

She drew in a suffocating breath. 'What a thing to say to me! I haven't!'

'Not deliberately, perhaps, but what does that matter? The great thing is, you *have*!'

She was struck into complete silence and he ignored her, turning the car off the main road and climbing up a long driveway that had been obscured by the denseness and height of the trees. Then they were coming on the house and she could find no parallel in her mind for the way it affected her. It had gone beyond today. It was tomorrow. Her eyes filled with tears and she bit on her lip, feeling her emotionally control slip from her.

He looked at her very hard and direct, seeing the shimmering tears. 'Natalie!' he said under his breath.

His eyes, like blue flame, reached for her and she let out a soft, shuddering breath. 'I don't know you at all, do I?'

'I don't think so. But you will!'

Form and function in the purest sense! The house stood on a hill in isolated splendour, looking way out across the Gulf, but it would have been outstanding in virtually any setting. Lang displayed a rare gift, and the whole man, the man she loved, came sharply into focus. She might try to find some life without him, but quite simply she could not. The thought was only surfacing in her subconscious mind, like some fantastic somersault. She couldn't explain now how she had been with him or why she had done it. Her rejection of him was, in fact, a fantasy. Their affinity had gone beyond the point of closeness. They thought, as it were, as one, yet she still had to come a little way further out of her unique wilderness.

The day was changing, amethyst invading the gold of late afternoon, altering the mood of the vast landscape. Natalie was changing too, going very quietly now by his side. They paused at the front exterior of the house and Lang said in a gentle, amused tone:

'This isn't the classic situation, Natalie, nor is it the result of a scheming mind, but Magda doesn't appear to be home!' He reached for her hand as though she might quickly run away and drew her beside him. 'Quite aptly, however, she seems to have left a note.'

The white scrap of paper with its ragged torn edges looked quite alien in the stunning setting of the brass knocker on the massive double front door, carved in decorative panels. Lang unfolded it and Natalie read over his arm, her heart pounding. Magda had obviously been in a hurry, or a black, decisive scrawl was habitual to her. The note read:

'Darling Lang, Molly in need of urgent counselling—*again*!!! Don't be cross. I swear I won't give her more than an hour of my time. Go in!'

It was signed with a flamboyant M.

'Molly, my God!' Lang sighed, and his eyebrows drew together in an irritable frown which inexplicably cleared like magic. 'Molly is a case, a woman with a frightful imagination—and the drink doesn't help. Margaret Sinclair, the singer,' he explained. 'The only reason I'm telling you that is that as a friend of Magda's you would have to know and understand. Molly simply won't stop until there's not a dreg, not a drop in the bottle. Without Magda, who's too soft for her own good, I think she'd go clear off her rocker. The pity of it, and all that remains of a great talent. She had everything going for her—everything! Ah well, what the devil are we waiting for? Let's go in!'

'It seems to be very thoroughly bolted to me,' Natalie suggested.

'What's this, then?' Lang reached behind her and produced a key from one of the two tall planters of Emperor of Russia camellias with their large glossy green leaves. 'Magda, brilliant artist that she is, is exactly like other women when it comes to hiding keys—always the most conspicuous place!'

'Is this really all right?' she asked dreamily, as he threw open one side of the carved timber door and touched his hand to a switch. There were no conventional light fittings or traditional or contemporary chandeliers, yet the whole beautiful, two-storied living room sprang into life. Natalie walked ahead of him over the glistening polished ceramic tiles of the floor. They were ebony like the great Steinway that angled into one wall.

It was a musician's house, acoustically perfect, where music could expand and soar up to the great timbered ceiling with its outstanding architectural detailing. The magnificent custom-built sofas were all upholstered in the same soft suede, the colour of driftwood, and the Barcelona chairs placed opposite them on their shining chrome curves were a dark iridescent gold. Some high-powered hidden spotlights focused attention on the room's brilliant and important collection of modern art, introducing colour into an otherwise mono-chromatic scheme, for the linen draperies that swung back from the vast window walls were sand-coloured.

The whole design displayed virtuosity on a plane Natalie had hitherto never encountered. It looked wonderfully natural and right, yet she knew it demanded technical mastery. Two great treasures of the past in the form of life-size oriental Kuan Yins, their bare feet firmly planted on brass inlaid antique chests, flanked either side of the ceiling-high brick fireplace, its gleaming ceramic-tiled hearth supporting a great brass planter of white-blossoming azaleas, with the yellow gold of dahlias and chrysanthemums reflected in the polished ebony. Every piece in the room seemed to relate so that in the end, the very large room which Magda used fairly frequently for concerts and entertaining showed a perfect attention to scale. A superb bronze of a bird with outstretched wings was poised against one window, so completely natural it might have flown in from the trees.

It was a tour de force and she knew it. The thought of the man behind it, the thought of Lang, was like the sea crashing relentlessly against rock. She was being pulled under. She should never have come. She simply couldn't measure up to him. He was like that great sea that could sweep her away for ever. 'There's nothing I can say. Nothing!' she said like an exhausted, forlorn child, quite clearly on the verge of tears again.

'Why worry, I know how you feel. Let Magda show you the rest of the house, and Natalie, I'll do better than this—what you see here. Right now, I want you to myself!'

Oddly taut, he was somehow behind her, without warning lifting her clear of the ground, cradling her in his arms, as though he couldn't wait another day. She couldn't yield, but she was too stunned to resist.

'Don't fight me,' he said in a voice that filled her with giddy excitement. 'Not now. You've been quite cruel enough!' They were together in the soft corner of one of the immense sofas and he pressed her back against his shoulder. 'Just stay here with me and relax. I won't touch you, Natalie, I promise you. You'll have to beg me!'

Almost at a given signal, as exquisitely clean as a teardrop, came the opening notes of the F Minor Ballade of Chopin's. One of the greatest of all compositions for the piano, it began with a brief andante introduction, launching into a haunting, slow waltz, repeated again and again, in elaborately decorated form, heralding the enormous tranquillity of the major theme that developed into the most stupendous rhapsody; a passionate re-statement of the first slow waltz that ended with a coda of such technical bravura it would have terrified anyone but a virtuoso pianist.

This Magda Francks had been since the age of seventeen when she first began to make a name for herself in the country of her adoption, Australia. In the next few years she was to be introduced to all the concert halls of Europe and Asia. This triumphant interpretation divested of all sentimentality and thunderous with a true, ever-mounting passion was the fruit of her full maturity as an artist.

At the first notes of the introduction Natalie's body stiffened in apprehension. Chopin! the most romantic, the most poignant of them all. She could have screamed with the pain of it, then gradually her body began to relax and she lost herself in listening. Chopin had known bitter, bitter sorrow and ecstasy. No pain was unendurable. Morning followed the night. Her heart was throbbing, borne upward, her beauty abandoned to the music. Lang —well, she cared for him passionately, but she did not know he was devouring her with his eyes.

As though his need was greater than his promise he touched her throat, and she opened her eyes, blinded by the brilliance of his blue gaze.... That glass barrier that had protected her was shattering into a million sparkling fragments, even the music seemed far away. Lang and the expression in his eyes seemed to blot out everything.

'Blue the colour of heaven!' she said oddly. She thought she might faint, instead she put up her slender arms and encircled his head.

'Tell me how you feel?' he said tautly.

'I love you!' Her eyes, large and brilliant, flashed up at him.

'Are you sure?'

'I ache for you!'

'Natalie!' He tightened his hold on her, lifting her higher in his arms, then he parted her mouth with his own. It was like being seared by the sun with the rest of the world melting away from them. There was no one but the two of them and he was the most beautiful thing she had ever known. Her head was thrown back against his shoulder with the music rippling like molten silver around them. How could she start a new life without him? How could she live at all without this sweet burning hunger?

'Tell me you love me,' she said against his mouth.

His blue glimmering eyes still held a trace of mockery. 'I thought I was very thoroughly doing that. Yes, I love you, my stubborn little girl!' His strong clever hands cupped her face. 'And I look after my own. There you have it, Natalie, you're everything I want!'

Such a torrent of tenderness and passion was in his voice, she began to cry as if her heart would break.

'What is it, tell me?' Strain and anxiety was there now.

'I'm sorry!' She gripped his hands and pressed them against her face.

'Why are you crying?' he asked quietly, threading his hand through her hair.

'I don't know,' she said, turning to him for comfort. 'How stupidly I've been behaving, perhaps. Playing hide and seek with my own heart.'

He bent his head and gave her a swift, furious kiss. 'But you've come full circle, haven't you? You belong with me.'

'Yes!' she said. 'I respect you utterly. Father—he would have been happy about us, don't you think?'

'My darling, he knew! And soon for you if you'll let me, I'll make the whole world fall into shape again! I'm very single-minded about some things—

absolute. And Natalie, I can't live without you.'

The very first star began to glimmer through the leafy lattice work of the trees.

'Starlight, star bright, first star I've seen to-night....'

But Lang leaned over her and the rest of her wish was lost in a declaration of love.

romance is beautiful!

**and Harlequin Reader Service
is your passport to the
Heart of Harlequin**

Harlequin is the world's leading publisher of romantic fiction novels. If you enjoy the mystery and adventure of romance, then you will want to keep up to date on all of our new monthly releases—eight brand new Romances and four Harlequin Presents.

If you are interested in catching up on exciting and valuable back issues, Harlequin Reader Service offers a wide choice of best-selling novels reissued for your reading enjoyment.

If you want a truly jumbo read and a money-saving value, the Harlequin Omnibus offers three intriguing novels under one cover by one of your favorite authors.

To find out more about Harlequin, the following information will be your passport to the Heart of Harlequin.

collection editions

**Rare Vintage Romance
From Harlequin**

The Harlequin Collection editions have been chosen
from our 400 through 899 series, and comprise some of
our earliest and most sought-after titles. Most of the
novels in this series have not been available since the
original publication and are available now in beautifully
redesigned covers.

When complete, these unique books will comprise the
finest collection of vintage romance novels available.
You will treasure reading and owning this delightful
library of beautiful love stories for many years to come.

For further information, turn to the back of this book and
return the INFORMATION PLEASE coupon.

the omnibus

A Great Idea! Three great romances by the same author, in one deluxe paperback volume.

A Great Value! Almost 600 pages of pure entertainment for only $1.95 per volume.

Essie Summers

Bride in Flight (#933)
... begins on the eve of Kirsty's wedding with the strange phone call that changed her life. Blindly, instinctively Kirsty ran — but even New Zealand wasn't far enough to avoid the complications that followed!

Postscript to Yesterday (#1119)
... Nicola was dirty, exasperated and a little bit frightened. She was in no shape after her amateur mechanics on the car to meet any man, let alone Forbes Westerfield. He was the man who had told her not to come.

Meet on My Ground (#1326)
... is the story of two people in love, separated by pride. Alastair Campbell had money and position — Sarah Macdonald was a girl with pride. But pride was no comfort to her at all after she'd let Alastair go!

Jean S. MacLeod

The Wolf of Heimra (#990)
... Fenella knew that in spite of her love for the island, she had no claim on Heimra yet — until an heir was born. These MacKails were so sure of themselves; they expected everything to come their way.

Summer Island (#1314)
... Cathie's return to Loch Arden was traumatic. She knew she was clinging to the past, refusing to let it go. But change was something you thought of happening in other places — never in your own beloved glen.

Slave of the Wind (#1339)
... Lesley's pleasure on homecoming and meeting the handsome stranger quickly changed to dismay when she discovered that he was Maxwell Croy — the man whose family once owned her home. And Maxwell was determined to get it back again.

Susan Barrie

Marry a Stranger (#1034)
...if she lived to be a hundred, Stacey knew she'd never be more violently in love than she was at this moment. But Edouard had told her bluntly that he would never fall in love with her!

Rose in the Bud (#1168)
...One thing Cathleen learned in Venice: it was highly important to be cautious when a man was a stranger and inhabited a world unfamiliar to her. The more charm he possessed, the more wary she should be!

The Marriage Wheel (#1311)
...Admittedly the job was unusual — lady chauffeur to Humphrey Lestrode; and admittedly Humphrey was high-handed and arrogant. Nevertheless Frederica was enjoying her work at Farthing Hall. Then along came her mother and beautiful sister, Rosaleen, to upset everything.

Violet Winspear

Beloved Tyrant (#1032)
...Monterey was a beautiful place to recuperate. Lyn's job was interesting. Everything, in fact, would have been perfect, Lyn Gilmore thought, if it hadn't been for the hateful Rick Corderas. He made her feel alive again!

Court of the Veils (#1267)
...In the lush plantation on the edge of the Sahara, Roslyn Brant tried very hard to remember her fiancé and her past. But the bitter, disillusioned Duane Hunter refused to believe that she ever was engaged to his cousin, Armand.

Palace of the Peacocks (#1318)
...Suddenly the island, this exotic place that so recently had given her sanctuary, seemed an unlucky place rather than a magical one. She must get away from the cold palace and its ghost — and especially from Ryk van Helden.

Isobel Chace

The Saffron Sky (#1250)
...set in a tiny village skirting the exotic Bangkok, Siam, the small, nervous Myfanwy Jones realizes her most cherished dream, adventure and romance in a far-off land. Two handsome men determine to marry her, but both have the same mysterious reason....

A Handful of Silver (#1306)
...in exciting Rio de Janeiro, city of endless beaches and skyscraper hotels, a battle of wits is waged between Madelaine Delahaye, Pilar Fernandez, the jealous fiancée of her childhood friend, and her handsome, treacherous cousin — Luis da Maestro....

The Damask Rose (#1334)
...Vicki Tremaine flies to the heady atmosphere of Damascus to meet Adam Templeton, fiancé of the rebellious Miriam. But alas, as time passes, Vicki only becomes more attracted to this young Englishman with the steel-like personality...

information please

**All the Exciting News from
Under the Harlequin Sun**

It costs you nothing to receive our news bulletins and
intriguing brochures. From our brand new releases to our
money-saving 3-in-1 omnibus and valuable best-selling
back titles, our information package is sure to be a hit.
Don't miss out on any of the exciting details. Send for
your Harlequin INFORMATION PLEASE package today.